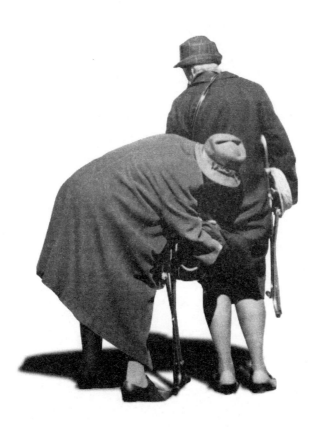

**Bridget Golightly** is eighty-nine years old. She won the 100 m, 800 m, triple jump and solo synchronised swimming events in the 1968 Mexico Olympic Games. Highlights of her sparkling stage and film career include two Academy Awards as Best Supporting Actress for *Little Dorrit* and *Rocky V*, and her much-lauded Titania against Sir John Gielgud's Bottom. Bridget is also a Nobel Prize-winning mathematician, renowned poet and international peace-keeper, and represented the United Kingdom in the 1959 Eurovision Song Contest with 'Boom-bang-a-ting-a-ling on a String'. When she's not busy bringing joy to the world, she likes to relax by drinking a nice cup of tea.

**Joan Hardcastle** is eighty-six years old, comes from Yorkshire and doesn't believe a word Bridget says. Except the bit about the tea.

Bridget Golightly &
        Joan Hardcastle

# BRIDGET &
# JOAN'S
# DIARY

Mad about
The Toy Boy

ONEWORLD

A Oneworld Book

First published by Oneworld Publications 2013

Copyright © @BridgetandJoan, 2013

The moral right of @BridgetandJoan to be identified as the
author of this work has been asserted by them in accordance
with the Copyright, Designs and Patents Act 1988

ISBN 978-1-78074-437-7
ISBN 978-1-78074-438-4 (eBook)

Typeset by Tetragon, London
Printed and bound by CPI Group (UK) Ltd, Croydon, CR0 4YY

Oneworld Publications
10 Bloomsbury Street
London WC1B 3SR
England

*For Harry and Adrian –*
*our two favourite toy boys.*

# NEW YEAR'S RESOLUTIONS

Bridget 👓

**I will not:**

- Drink sherry before eleven in the morning (except on Sundays. Fine to drink Tia Maria as it's essentially coffee).

- Spend all of my pension on the morning I get it.

- Be quite so talkative. Will instead be quiet, like the mysterious screen goddess I am.

- Waste money on: anti-ageing creams, bust-firming creams, books with no pictures, pregnancy tests, trousers you can't pull on, push-up bras, temporary tattoos (as getting real one), deposits on 18–30 holidays.

- Be quite so experimental with my hair colour (may put gentlemen off).

- Pretend to collapse in post office in order to push to front of queue.

- Fantasise about Father O'Brien (or his choirboys).

- Sing during bingo (seems to make people angry – no idea why).
- Order large items from Shopping Channel just so I can flirt with postman.

**I will:**

- Embrace the feminine glory of my sixty-five-year-old womanhood.
- Appear on stage one last time (to draw the curtain on my sparkling theatrical career with one final, unforgettable performance).
- Meet the love of my life. (No intention of spending another Valentine's Day with Joan.)
- Fly in a hot-air balloon.
- Swim with dolphins.
- Get one of those marvellous pink-rabbit hand blenders. Like the ones I've seen on the late-night shopping channel.
- See the Northern Lights.
- Get a tattoo (something tasteful and subtle, like small white rose. Or Julio Iglesias).
- Go on a road trip.
- Spend less time with Joan (she really needs to stand on her own two feet).

# Joan 👓

**I will not:**

- Talk to Bridget if she's drunk at breakfast.
- Lend money to Bridget when she's frittered away her pension.
- Roll my eyes every time Bridget tells one of her 'true stories' about her past. Not every time, at least.

**I will:**

- Complete my fifty-thousand-piece Serial Killers Through the Ages jigsaw.
- Set aside morning to organise my wardrobe.
- Set aside month to organise Bridget's wardrobe.
- Be more tolerant of Bridget's singing.
- Be more tolerant of Bridget's dancing.
- Be more tolerant of Bridget (although I've no intention of spending Valentine's Day with her again).
- Check Bridget is wearing her incontinence pants every morning.
- Organise sponsored bridge evening to raise money for new dining-room carpet (see above).

- Remind Bridget that she's eighty-nine. On a daily basis.
- If all of above fail, take up smoking or hard drugs.

# JANUARY

## Tuesday 1st

Cups of tea drunk – 23 (v bad)

Teabags used – 4 (v good)

Trips to toilet – 12 (average)


Well, this is a new experience! Starting the New Year writing in a diary. (And not having a hangover – not for the want of trying, mind you. I swear that new care-home manager, Mrs Sharples, waters down the advocaat.) I haven't kept a diary since I was a little girl. It was a present from Joan. Still, I suppose it's better than last year's diary. That was already filled in by a couple called Anne and Frank. A bit weird, two people writing in the same diary, if you ask me. I wouldn't have minded but it's not as if they did anything worth writing about. As far as I could tell they just spent all their time in their loft conversion, keeping really quiet so they didn't annoy their neighbours. Although Germans can be terrible complainers.

Pleased to see that Bridget's actually using the diary I got her for Christmas. I knew it was a good idea. Time she got her thoughts and her life in order. Don't know where I'd be without this one of mine. Though she shouldn't leave it just lying around for anyone to read. I always keep mine securely locked in my bedside cabinet. I should tell Bridget to do the same… although, actually, I might not. Just in case. Suppose I should be glad she's using it at all. I don't think she even looked at that copy of Anne Frank's *Diary* that I got her last year.

## Wednesday 2nd

What a lovely time at the day centre with Joan. Had a little sing-song and fish and chips for tea. My favourite! Shame I lost my teeth.

Awful time at the day centre with Bridget. She insisted on singing. Had to turn my hearing aid off. Cheered myself up by hiding her teeth.

## Thursday 3rd

I think I'll make a nice cup of tea for me and Joan. I just need to find the sugar. And the milk. And the cups. I like my tea like I like my men. Strong, sweet and dark.

I like my tea like I like my men too. Still warm.

## Friday 4th

Went to the January sales today! It was lovely, just like the Blitz all over again. Sat around for hours, me entertaining everyone with my specially extended wartime medley. For once, Joan encouraged me. She reckoned my singing was making the queue shorter. When the doors finally opened, I rushed straight in. Joan says you need a strategy for these kinds of things – she reckons it's best to make a list of the things you need and stick to it. I say, where's the fun in that? Life's for living as far as I'm concerned. I like to take in the atmosphere and really enjoy myself. Plus, as I keep reminding her, you can use one of those little plastic cards these days so you're not actually spending any money. I've got loads of them.

That's it. That's the last time I go to the sales with Bridget. It was like the Blitz all over again. Bridget was like a doodlebug, whizzing around the place causing mayhem and destruction. I told her that you have to approach these things with a clear plan but does she listen to me? Goodness only knows what she's bought. And how much it all cost! I, on the other hand, restricted myself to just the one purchase: a nice, sensible cardigan like the one Gloria Hunniford wears in the life-insurance commercial. But without the free pen.

## Saturday 5th

Twelfth Night tonight. Everyone else insists it's tomorrow – something to do with Jesus – but we always took the decorations down on the fifth when I was a little girl and you can't take any chances with this kind of thing. Well, if nobody's going to help I suppose I'll just have to do it on my own. And if I have to eat all the remaining chocolate baubles myself, that's just the price I'll have to pay.

6.30 p.m. Bridget got it into her head that we had to take down all the Christmas decorations tonight or we'd go to hell. There's no arguing with her when she's in that mood so, for a quiet life, I went off to borrow Mr Gooch's telescopic ladder. I'm not entirely sure why he's got a telescopic ladder. Or those night-vision goggles, for that matter. He claims he's in the local neighbourhood watch but I have it on good authority that he was suspended last year for being 'a little too observant'. Anyway, my back was turned for just five minutes and Bridget was there on the windowsill in her chiffon nightdress and tartan slippers, trying to grab the end of a crêpe-paper garland and wobbling like a bowlful of jelly. Luckily, Father O'Brien was in giving the last rites to Mrs Mountjoy, so I got him to keep an eye on Bridget while I fetched a duvet to catch her in. Eventually I managed to find a king-size one and braced myself…

## Sunday 6th

Went to visit Joan in hospital today. Took a few things to cheer her up.

Grapes – 1 bunch
Lucozade – 1 bottle

*Take a Break* magazine – 1

Thanks from Joan for the above – zero

Things Bridget brought into hospital to 'cheer me up':

Grapes – zero (Bridget ate them all)

Lucozade – 1 sip (Bridget drank the rest)

*Take a Break* magazine – 1 (I prefer the *Racing Post*)

Bridget's flirts with doctor – 5

## Monday 7th

Joan came out of hospital today so I created a special 'welcome home' dance especially for her. I based it loosely on Gypsy Rose Lee. She was so overcome she had to go for a lie down.

The other residents didn't seem to enjoy Bridget dancing around the lounge in her knickers but I thought she was hysterical. That's why I slapped her.

## Tuesday 8th

I woke up this morning to a magical winter wonderland! I was so excited that I dashed straight out into the garden after breakfast. I'm going to build a special snow sculpture of Joan to show her how much her friendship means to me.

Temperature – invigorating!

Vest – lacy

Cardigans – zero (so frumpy)

Fun level – 10/10 (v good)

Bridget just tramped slush all over my carpet. She said she wanted to make a 'Snowjoan' but there wasn't enough snow. I said she'd make a good snow angel. All she needed to do was lie down and wait for hypothermia to set in.

Temperature – -2 degrees Celsius (28.4 degrees Fahrenheit)

Vest – thermal

Cardigans – several

Fun level – -2

## Wednesday 9th

Just a slice of toast for tea today. I do like cottage pie but these days it always seems to give me the runs, so Joan had mine.

Poor Bridget. She thinks cottage pie gives her the runs. She's no idea I put laxatives in her tea. Still, waste not want not.

## Thursday 10th

Had a lovely trip to the supermarket with Joan.

Sherry – 5 bottles

Luxury Belgian triple-chocolate macaroons – 4 packets

Number of times fell into chest freezer – 3

Had a stressful trip to the supermarket with Bridget.

Teabags – 160

Value custard creams – 1 packet

Number of displays knocked over by Bridget's trolley – 3

Number of items Bridget attempted to purchase at '6 items or less' checkout – 38

Number of pennies Bridget used to pay for shopping – 649

Number of times retrieved Bridget from chest freezer – 2

## Friday 11th

Poor Mr Sargent's funeral today. What a shock. One minute he's a vibrant, virile, medically assisted gentleman, the next he's entirely rigid. They reckon it was his heart. That only leaves Mr Gooch now. Slim pickings for a woman in the prime of her life. The only glint in his eye is his astigmatism. At least Joan's happy. As social occasions go, funerals are her favourite. And she doesn't have to buy any new clothes, as all hers are black already.

Ham sandwiches consumed – 2

Sherries, small – 1

Compliments about my cheerful red dress – 3

Mr Sargent's funeral this morning. I do like a good funeral. Far better class of sandwich. The poor soul would have been 100 – if he'd lived another twelve years. Apparently he asked to be scattered over the place where he spent his happiest moments – but Bridget wasn't keen on having ash all over her duvet.

Ham sandwiches consumed by Bridget – 11

Sherries consumed by Bridget – 8

Disapproving looks at Bridget's red dress – several

## Sunday 13th

What a wonderful day. I don't know exactly where I am but I feel like I've been walking for miles! Poor Joan must be struggling to keep up – I wonder where she can have got to? Oh well, I'd better keep going…

What a wonderful day. Enjoying a lovely, peaceful Sunday lunch in the Pig and Whistle. I must remember to pick Bridget up from IKEA when I'm done.

## Tuesday 15th

Nice day. Gave Joan my Christmas Club money to pay in at the post office. Spam and rice pudding for tea.

Nice day. Won ninety pounds on the scratchcard I got with Bridget's Christmas Club money. Lobster and champagne for tea.

## Friday 18th

Went for a check-up this morning. Joan insisted on tagging along even though I'm not the slightest bit nervous of anything medicinal. I had to let her come – the poor love never seems to know what to do with herself. I saw a new doctor today: Dr Turnbull. That's the fifth in as many weeks; I must be so popular they all want a go with me! Anyway, this one's got a lovely soothing voice and terribly muscular forearms. He said I've got nothing to worry about. Apparently, my hereditary weak bladder aside, I've got the body of a woman half my age. I shouldn't be surprised really – all that Olympic training was bound to have had an effect. If only Joan were so fit. Despite her size, she's really quite weak, the poor dear.

Bridget begged me to go with her to the doctor's surgery. I don't know why she's so worried. As I keep telling her, they're more scared of you than you are of them. Literally.

Dr Aziz was forced to take early retirement with his nerves and Dr Hardiman needed a precautionary tetanus shot after her last visit. After yet another thorough medical, this latest doctor said that a woman of her age needed more physical activity so I volunteered to help. I moved her wardrobe in front of the toilet door.

## Saturday 19th

I fancy a bit of Saturday-night fun for a change so I've told Joan we should go out and pick up a couple of nice gentlemen and go off gallivanting.

I'm all for a bit of fun but, as I told Bridget, even if we could pick up a couple of gentlemen, we'd never be able to fit them on our mobility scooters.

## Sunday 20th

I do look forward to Sunday bingo. I usually go with Joan but she must have forgotten to knock on my door today.

Managed to sneak out to bingo without Bridget for once. I wouldn't mind but when we arrive together, the caller always shouts out 'Two fat ladies'. To which Bridget always responds 'One-and-a-half, actually' and gives me one of her ever-so-loving can't-quite-reach-all-the-way-round cuddles.

## Wednesday 23rd

Went to the day centre this afternoon. I had a lovely time in the art class. They said they were full but I managed to persuade them to squeeze me in. I even managed to convince Joan to come along. She pretended she didn't want to but I know she enjoyed it really. She's not so creatively minded as me so I booked her into something more practical – mobility-scooter maintenance.

Horrendous time at the day centre this afternoon. Bridget barged her way into the life-drawing class. I told her they already had a model but, before I could stop her, she was straddling the plinth with her Crimplene dress at her feet and nothing but a bunch of rubber grapes to cover her modesty. They really need to get a bigger bunch.

## Friday 25th

Goodness, I'm exhausted! I need a good lie down. I feel like I've been up and down these stairs all day.

Poor Bridget. Someone accidentally swapped the television remote with her stairlift controller. Can't imagine who…

## Wednesday 30th

Two o'clockish. I can hardly contain myself – it's pantomime day! My favourite: *Jack and the Beanstalk*! Joan's excited too, although she's better at hiding it. Just waiting for the orchestra to strike up and the fire curtain to be raised (I've no idea why they still have one of those now the theatre's no smoking. Tradition, I suppose). I wonder if Brendan O'Bannon will be wearing the reindeer jumper I sent him? I'm sure he will, he's such a lovely young man. I don't know how many signed photos he must have sent me.

2.17 p.m. Can't believe I let Bridget talk me into coming to this thing. If there's one thing I can't bear it's enforced jollity. If the Lord had meant us to be jolly, he'd have given us something to be jolly about. Of course, Bridget's in a proper tizzy, as usual. You'd never think she'd spent forty years on the stage herself. If she did. She keeps rocking to and fro on her seat and mumbling something about this being her last chance. I told her she should've gone before we left the home.

Evening. Back from the theatre. Still trying to take it all in. I can't believe it – Brendan O'Bannon wore MY jumper! AND he called me up on stage to lead the sing-song! Well, I say 'me' – he actually called for several volunteers. I don't know what's wrong with children these days; they just don't seem to be bothered. Anyway, I've done it. I've fulfilled my first resolution. And, if I do say so myself, I really lit up that stage.

7.30 p.m. Back from the theatre. Still trying to take it all in. One minute Jack's calling for volunteers to help with some song, the next, Bridget's standing up there by his side, a mass of small children lying in the aisles in her wake. I remember one verse of 'If You're Happy and You Know It', then Jack's jumper lighting up like the Blackpool Illuminations, then the expression of surprise on Jack's face as his jumper catches fire and the gasps from the audience as he careers into the pantomime cow. After that, it's all a bit of a blur...

## Thursday 31st

Pantomime final inventory

Casualties:

- Children (trampled by Bridget) – 12
- Pantomime cow (front half) – 1
- Much-loved Irish entertainer – 1
- Pantomime cow (back half) – 1
- Mint imperials – 5

Fatalities:

- Beanstalk – 1
- Grade 2-listed eighteenth-century theatre roof – 1

Fire engines – 6

Entertainment value – 10

# FEBRUARY

## Friday 1st

Looks like being an exciting month. Mrs Sharples is introducing all sorts of new activities. Apparently we're getting a Scrabble board, a chess set, a box of dominoes and one of those fancy new computers. She says it's very important at our age that we keep our minds and bodies active. She's even put one of those new Paganini makers in the lounge. I hope she isn't expecting us to make our own sandwiches too.

Bridget's very excited about all these new activities, although she's not really sure why we're getting a computer. I explained that care homes often use computer games to keep their residents physically active. That's why old people smell of Wii.

## Saturday 2nd

Bridget's just asked me to look at that new panini maker for her. She said she'd turned the thing on two hours ago and it was still barely lukewarm. Gave it a thorough examination. Removed partially melted slice of Emmental. Informed Bridget that it was a laptop computer.

## Thursday 7th

I have just one guilty pleasure. I like to have a nice custard cream with my morning cup of tea.

I have just one guilty pleasure. I like to stand on crowded buses in the hope of getting touched inappropriately.

## Monday 11th

Mrs Sharples has just given us all a series of mental tests to assess the effectiveness of her new regime.

My results:

Mental recall test – 94%

Reflex test – 0.7 seconds

Logic test – 100%

Thoroughly enjoyed Mrs Sharples's tests this morning. I don't know how I've done, but I must have beaten Joan.

My results:

Mental recall test – 23%

Reflex test – half an hour

Logic test – 0%

## Tuesday 12th

Very excited about the pancake race today! I wasn't going to enter, as I've beaten Joan to the finishing line for the last four years running and really wanted to give the poor old dear a chance for once. It's surprising really, you'd think Joan would be perfectly built for pancake tossing with her great big docker's wrists – mine are so irritatingly slender, delicate and feminine. I'm not at all competitive, but in the end she wouldn't hear of me not defending my title, so I gave in. I'll probably let her win. Mind you, I wouldn't want to disappoint the crowds – not after last year's run when I made the national news! I've done a little bit of practice, mind, just to keep my hand in. Mr Gooch says it's all in the wrist action and he's been helping me to streamline my tossing technique.

Eggs used – 3

Flour – 4 oz

Milk – half a pint

Pancakes made – 6

Pancakes successfully tossed – 6

Dreading the pancake race today, especially if it's anything like last year when Bridget managed to throw batter all over the crowd and tripped up, elbowed and kicked every poor soul in her path. Five residents had to be rushed to A & E with life-changing injuries and Mrs Dibby's pacemaker stopped twice (although it turned out that the batteries needed changing). She even made the national news – the Pancake Prowler. Mind you, she's always been competitive, has our Bridget. As a child she used to stamp on my fingers while I was doing handstands. She's been training with Mr Gooch as though tossing were an Olympic event, which for him it probably is. Goodness knows how much batter they've wasted. As I told Bridget, the whole point of Shrove Tuesday is to clear your cupboards of flour, eggs and milk before you fast for lent, not bulk panic-buy them!

Eggs Bridget used – 4 dozen

Flour – 3 lbs

Milk – 5 pints

Pancakes made – 48

Pancakes dropped – 21

Pancakes stuck to ceiling – 27

Gallons of emulsion required to repaint kitchen – 16

## Wednesday 13th

Ten o'clock. I've certainly no intention of spending another Valentine's Day with Joan so I'm taking extreme action: I'm going to hunt out my little black book. I might not have used it since 1963 but from what I remember there were quite a few hunks in there, all of whom I'm sure would be more than happy to spend a romantic evening with a certain blonde bombshell. I'm expecting some pretty spectacular results.

Results:

Moved – 23

Married – 16

Deceased – 19

Bedridden – 2

Busy that evening – 12

Left the country – 2

Entered priesthood – 3

Didn't answer phone – 5

Did answer phone but quickly put it down again – 7

Missing, presumed drowned – 25

Half past eleven. Oh dear, looks like I'm stuck with Joan for Valentine's Day again after all. Oh well, I suppose I'd better make the most of it. I couldn't face spending the evening in, watching Mr Gooch adjusting his unmentionables. I'd better book a restaurant, I suppose…

11.36 a.m. Oh dear, looks like I'm stuck with Bridget for Valentine's Day again after all. And after I spent two hours helping her find her 'little' black book. I only hope she doesn't book anything too cosy…

Two o'clock. Found a restaurant with a spare table at last. It wasn't easy, this close to Valentine's Day. I promised Joan I wouldn't book anywhere romantic and I know how she likes her unusual food so I think I've outdone myself this time. I found a new Libyan restaurant in the Yellow Pages – that should be right up her alley. And I made it clear when I booked that we were both women, so there shouldn't be any confusion – even if Joan forgets to shave.

## Thursday 14th

Eleven o'clock. Such an enchanting evening! What a beautiful restaurant, all candlelit and romantic. That young Mediterranean waiter with the tight trousers definitely took a shine to me. If only I were two or three years younger. And although he was talking in some fancy foreign language, it didn't matter because he was speaking the international language: love.

11.12 p.m. Such a bizarre evening. The restaurant was so dark I could barely see my hand in front of my face. Luckily my O level in European modern languages meant I could talk to the waiter otherwise I'd have had to listen to Bridget all night. My Italian's a little shaky but it didn't matter because he was speaking the international language: football.

Even so, it was still an extremely uncomfortable experience. The abundance of rose petals, gypsy violinists and erotic baguettes did little to ease my mind. But it was only when the maître d' made a grand announcement that the full picture became clear.

'Good evening, ladies and ladies. Welcome to our very special Valentine's dinner. We hope you will all have a truly memorable romantic evening tonight at Casa DeGeneres!'

I really must take Bridget for an eye test as soon as possible. Libyan restaurant, my foot! It was a lesbian restaurant. Of course, it didn't help when Bridget insisted on ordering oysters for our starters and one bowl of spaghetti between us so that we could eat it like Lady and the Tramp. Never again!

## Sunday 17th

Cornered by those smug marrieds, Alf and Irene Potter, at the breakfast table. As usual they were nagging me about my marital status, about how proud they are to be the only couple in the home and how the rest of us need to pull our fingers out and find partners 'because our body clocks are ticking and soon we're going to need someone to push our wheelchairs and wipe the drool from our chins. And we don't want to end up sad, lonely wrinkletons with nothing to look forward to but dying alone.' In the end I had to go up to my room and leave them to go back to screaming and throwing mugs of hot tea at each other.

## Monday 18th

I must say, this Internet thing is amazing! Joan's been showing it to me on the laptop computer – she said it might keep me out of mischief, the cheeky beggar. I didn't realise you could send letters on it – and without a stamp!

Helped Bridget to open an email account. Figured that way she can spend half the day pestering the rest of the world instead of me. It's taken her a little while to get used to it. Just popped in to see how she was doing and had to remove half a dozen stamps from the computer screen.

## Tuesday 19th

Just spent a lovely morning in the library. It's the perfect place to keep warm on a cold day like this for nothing.

Just had a call to collect Bridget from the library. Apparently they have some rule about people burning books.

## Wednesday 20th

Almost a disaster – we nearly went out without our sticks. We don't need them for walking with, just for poking small children.

## Thursday 21st

I think I'm really getting the hang of this email thingummybob now. I've sent letters to all of my friends and relatives. I haven't had any back yet but maybe they're using second class.

## Friday 22nd

Hooray! I got my first email. From one of my relatives – who knew I was related to Nigerian royalty? And such a nice man too, dear Uncle Adetokunbo. He even says he wants to send me a million pounds, would you believe? All I need to do is send him a thousand pounds to sort out some legal documents or some such and he'll send it to me by return of post. I think I'll send him one of my jumpers too – don't want him thinking I'm taking advantage.

## Saturday 23rd

Went to one of those teeth-whitening places today. Joan's been giving me very strange looks – she's probably envious of my new smile!

Not sure what Bridget's been up to today, but she's come home wearing someone else's teeth.

## Sunday 24th

Just Googled something for the first time! Apparently you can find out anything you want with it. Joan showed me how – she says it's just like me asking her a question, only I don't have to wake her up in the middle of the night to do it. I must say, it's very impressive – just like a computer! I've been trying to get that bit under the toilet rim clean for ages and it's getting worse. All I had to do was type in the words 'urgent rimming' and it came up with over six million results. I wasn't too sure about some of them but in the end I found what I was looking for…

## Monday 25th

Ham salad for tea. It's so wafer thin since Mrs Sharples started using that new catering company, I can actually see the pattern of the plate through it!

Ham salad for tea. It's no wonder Bridget can only see the pattern on her plate. I ate her ham.

## Tuesday 26th

Bridget and I have had a little chat. She says she's beginning to feel the cold more now. Maybe I should let her inside for a few hours.

## Thursday 28th

Half past one. A new resident arrived today – Enid. A bit quiet. I expect it's only shyness. She just needs someone like me to jolly her along. I know what will work: my little medley of wartime favourites. That never fails to cheer people up.

1.32 p.m. A new resident arrived today. Checked her file while Mrs Sharples was out of the office. Apparently she's on suicide watch – she never recovered from losing her husband Cliff in the war. The poor man fell off a dirigible just off the coast of Dover – white as a sheet when they finally pulled him out, it said. Tried to top herself thirty-six times at her last home. They felt a change of scene might do her good. Can't imagine this place will help the poor woman – particularly if Bridget starts singing.

Half past eight. Enid's still very quiet, despite my singing. Still, I'm not going to give up until she cracks a smile. I know, I'll hit her with my all-time favourite, 'The White Cliffs of Dover'.

# MARCH

## Friday 1st

Hooray, Mrs Sharples has announced another exciting project this month. She wants us to film our reminiscences of the war to help stimulate our long-term memories. Joan's not too keen, but I think it's a wonderful idea. I've put myself forward as camerawoman and director. Oscars, here I come!

## Monday 4th

Lovely day reminiscing about the American soldiers we met during the war. They were all queuing up to jitterbug with me, you know. Joan was green with envy. She always said they were overpaid, oversexed and over here.

Bridget didn't jitterbug with any Americans during the war. She was always with me – sitting next to the toilets hand jiving.

## Wednesday 6th

Being a land girl during the war was magical. Strawberry picking in the sunshine. Sharing a laugh with lusty young farmers. Tables laden with pork pies, home-baked bread and freshly churned butter. Dancing the night away with handsome Americans – and bunking up in the hayloft.

Being a land girl during the war was diabolical. Shovelling cow dung in the rain. Getting slapped on the backside by toothless old farmers. Dry bread and pickled onions every mealtime. Doing the polka with Bridget in the cowshed and experimenting with lesbianism in the hayloft.

## Friday 8th

Better and better. Apparently I can put my films directly onto the computer and then anyone in the world can watch them. Mr Gooch showed me how to do it – he says he puts his own films on that Internet thingy all the time. He suggested that I should put mine on something called the YouTube (although he doesn't use it himself). I asked him why he didn't put his films on there but he just said that they were for a more specialist audience. Well, that's fine by me – the more people who see my masterpieces the better. That should really put that snooty Joan's nose out of joint!

Can't go anywhere without Bridget sticking that blooming camera in my face. I told her if she's got to film me at all, to do it from my left side, because my nose is slightly out of joint.

## Saturday 9th

Just put my first-ever film on that YouTube thingy. It's only me chatting to Joan about the rationing while she drinks some tea but it's already had a million viewers!

I can't understand why so many people want to see Bridget's boring video. Could it be the title she gave it: 'Two Old Ladies One Cup'?

## Wednesday 13th

Reminiscing about VJ Day with Joan – I'll never forget it. I was the young girl in that iconic photograph, dizzy with love and joy, in a sailor's arms in New York.

I'll never forget VJ Day. Bridget was dizzy with port and lemon in the Sailor's Arms in York.

## Friday 15th

Another YouTube hit! Three million people have watched my film about Joan on that old stairlift that needs oiling: Joan Takes It All the Way Up without Lubrication. Mr Gooch says I must have gone viral. I told him not to be so disgusting.

## Saturday 16th

A miracle! Managed to persuade Joan to go out with me on a Saturday night. What a classy venue: comfy sofas and half-price cocktails all night! Joan had a Long Island Nice Cup of Tea and I went for a Slow, Comfortable Walk around the Living Room.

Terrible evening! Sticky lino, disgusting drinks and Bridget chatting up every young man in the place. That's the last time I go to Grab a Grandson night!

# Sunday 17th

Joan's grandchildren came to visit again today. I don't know why she always tries to avoid them; they're delightful. They call me Nanna Bridget and make a big fuss of me. They play me their music on their little iProds – Sacha loves her gangster rap and Shane's into death metal. And their parents are lovely too. Joan's son, Philip, always gives me a friendly handshake and his wife Jane is looking much calmer since their youngest went to that teenage boot camp in Bosnia. There's never a dull moment. Almost makes me wish I'd had some of my own, but they just wouldn't have fitted in with my hectic stage and film career. I did contemplate having children when I neared my forties. I was aware time was running out if I wanted to take on any pregnant-housewife roles.

Suppose I'd better pop down and say hello to Philip and the family. I try to keep actual physical contact to a bare minimum. Over the years I've developed a number of effective strategies to minimise spending time with teenage grandchildren.

1. Knitting them Thomas the Tank Engine jumpers for their birthdays

2. Spitting on my handkerchief and dabbing vigorously at their cheeks

3. Deliberately mixing up their names

4. Asking them if they are courting

5. Giving them half-sucked boiled sweets

6. Asking them to help me when I go to the lavatory

I also have a strategy for dealing with middle-aged children: tell them I'm leaving all my money to the cat.

## Monday 18th

Quite a traumatic day. Somehow Enid managed to get hold of a gun. Apparently, she's got herself one of those new 3D printers and downloaded some files off an al-Qaeda website. She locked herself in Mrs Sharples's office, threatening to blow her own head off. It was a very tense afternoon – I barely got any of my jigsaw done. The police sent a trained negotiator, but just when it looked like he was beginning to get through to her, she placed the gun against the side of her head and pulled the trigger. Fortunately, she'd down-loaded the files for a water pistol so no harm was done. In fact, her hearing has never been better.

## Tuesday 19th

As you get older, losing friends is inevitable. So I've fitted Bridget with a tracking device for when she wanders off.

## Thursday 21st

A lovely spring day today. Took the bus out into the countryside to get a bit of peace and fresh air. Unfortunately, Bridget came too so I didn't get either. I wouldn't mind if she talked a bit of sense every now and then. The following is a severely edited transcription of the day's conversations.

Bridget: 'Are we nearly there yet?'

Bridget: 'Are we nearly there yet?'

Bridget: 'Are we nearly there yet?'

Bridget: 'I remember when all this was nothing but fields.'
Me: 'It still is nothing but fields.'
Bridget: 'No it isn't, there's a sheep.'

Bridget: 'Have you ever noticed how the longer you stare at a cloud, the more it starts to look like an animal?'

Me: 'You're still looking at a sheep.'

Bridget: 'Sheep are such stupid creatures – they just blindly follow each other wherever they go.'

Me: 'I'm over here, Bridget. You're talking to a sheep.'

Bridget: 'Are we nearly home yet?'

## Monday 25th

This online shopping is marvellous! You just click what you want to buy with your whatsit and tell it your address, and, as if by magic, the postman brings it a few days later. He's definitely got the hots for me. Whenever he looks at me I can feel him mentally unwrapping my parcels.

Self-help books – 3

Sparkly tops – 5

Melon baller gadget – 2 (Buy 1 Get 1 Free)

Electronic talking parrot – 1 (to keep Joan company)

Lusty looks from postman – 9

So much for Bridget's New Year's resolution about not flirting with the postman, poor man. It's bad enough that she keeps buying useless things off the Internet for herself – but why does she have to buy them for me too?

Broken talking parrot from eBay – 1 (present from Bridget)
Melon baller gadget – 1 (present from Bridget. BOGOF)

## Tuesday 26th

One of the care assistants found Mr Gooch stuffing Disney toys up himself last night. Of course, we had to take the Mickey out of him.

## Thursday 28th

Bridget's so forgetful these days. She's gone and left her glasses on the bus again. She forgot you're not allowed to drink sherry on public transport.

## Saturday 30th

Think I may have found a man; that should shut Alf and Irene up. He was in the back of the *Daily Herald*, of all places. I don't normally go in for these lonely-hearts ads but they've started a new section, Fantasy Flings. Looks far more my kind of thing. He's called Victor, he's 6 ft 2, and he's looking for a 'flexible playmate with GSOH and own transport' for something called 'role play'. Sounds terribly romantic – I can just picture us, standing on the deck of a cruise ship in the moonlight, me in my peach taffeta ballgown and him in a white tuxedo, whispering sweet nothings in my good ear. Or riding a silver stallion across the blazing desert sands to his silk-strewn Bedouin tent. As luck would have it, he's invited me to the Fantasy Flings Easter Bunnies and Bishops Sausage Sizzle at Middleton Manor tonight. I've told him I've got a car, so I hope he doesn't spot me getting off the bus. Joan isn't sure about me meeting somebody so soon – she does fuss – so I've let her come with me so she doesn't feel left out. I've got a good feeling about this. Looking my dazzling best, mingling with fellow theatricals and finding my soulmate in a wonderful world of imagination!

Well, Bridget's outfit certainly leaves nothing to the imagination. I hope she's going to be all right at this sausage-fest, or whatever it is. Bunnies and bishops – all sounds a bit odd to me. She's surprisingly nervous for once, so I've agreed to go with her on the bus and wait for a few minutes in case he doesn't turn up. Which, if he's got any sense, he won't.

## Sunday 31st

Well, that was some evening last night. I stayed just long enough to watch Bridget's show-stopping entrance – all eyes were on her as she made her way through the crowd of sexy bunny girls and naughty bishops. From the moment she entered, she was the centre of attention – she clearly had something the other women didn't. A Bugs Bunny costume and a bag of carrots. She finally arrived home at three o'clock this morning. In the back of a police car. Apparently, they caught her in their headlights halfway home and picked her up for jaywalking and trying to bribe a police officer with a root vegetable. Honestly, I'd been worried sick all night. Well, at least until the shipping forecast.

I can't believe it, how embarrassing! I tried to brazen my way through the evening but after the umpteenth kinky bishop asked me what was up, doc? and Victor's absence became more and more noticeable, I decided to cut my losses, finish my eighth glass of champagne and head home.

# MARCH

As I trudged down the driveway, trying not to trip over my big feet, all I could hear was a chorus of 'Th-th-th-that's all, folks!' ringing in my giant ears.

# APRIL

## Monday 1st

Oooh terrific! April Fool's Day! My favourite day of the year, apart from Christmas Day, my birthday and any day we have rice pudding for tea. Joan and I always go out and play tricks on the local community. They love it when we throw powdered eggs at their houses and ring their doorbells and walk away slowly. We even have a best-trickster competition between us. Of course, I usually win as I have by far the more creative mind. My best joke was probably the year I tied Joan's shoelaces together. Unfortunately my hip locked and I couldn't get back up again. I must have been down there for three days but I don't think she noticed.

Oh terrific. April Fool's Day. My least favourite day of the year, apart from Christmas Day, Bridget's birthday and every day we have moussaka for tea. Every year it's the same: Bridget attempting to trick me with some desperate joke she got from the *Beano*. And she always insists I join in the 'fun' even though I'd rather be in bed with a severe chill. I suppose my best joke was the year I squirted superglue into her artificial hip while she was trying to tie my shoelaces together.

## Tuesday 2nd

Pasta for dinner. Joan says it's called tagliatelle. What a tongue-twister!

Pasta for dinner. It's penne but I've told Bridget it's tagliatelle. Just to see her teeth fall out when she tries to pronounce it.

## Wednesday 3rd

Mrs Dibby died during the patchwork class this afternoon. But she did manage to complete her cushion. So at least that softened the blow for her son. That leaves Ivy the oldest resident at ninety-nine. She's survived two world wars, nineteen prime ministers and Bridget's singing.

## Thursday 4th

It's Joan's birthday tomorrow. She pretends she doesn't like celebrating it and always says she doesn't want any fuss but I know that deep down she does really so I always make sure I pull out all the stops, whether it's a firework display or a Chippendale jumping out of a giant cake. I know that under that expression of sheer horror she's secretly over the moon – who wouldn't be? I would be but Joan's not the sort to organise anything like that for me. On my last birthday, she got me a subscription to the high-fibre food-of-the-month club. This month it's figs. On the other hand, I always put a great deal of thought into my gifts.

My best presents for Joan:

1. Pink chiffon baby-doll nightie

2. Tickle-me-Elmo

3. Necklace with heart-shaped silver locket containing a lock of my hair

My birthday tomorrow, as Bridget has kindly reminded me.

My best presents from Bridget:

1. A pencil

I dread to think what she's got me this year. Hopefully it'll be something I can do in peace.

## Friday 5th

Gave Joan her birthday present first thing this morning. It's one of those new iTelephones that you see all the young people using. I must say, this special Internet 'money' is terribly handy; all you have to do is put in your credit-card details and you can buy what you like for free! I got one for her and one for me – that way we can be in constant contact! She was so touched, she was close to tears, the big old silly. I haven't managed to figure out how to work it yet – I've tried calling the operator but I haven't had any luck. Never mind, I'm sure Joan will be more than happy to show me. It'll be a nice break from the monotony of that awful jigsaw of hers.

## Saturday 6th

I've found the operator! Joan showed me which button to press. Sounds very nice, too – called Cyril, apparently. Funny name for a girl if you ask me. Joan says you can get these things called apps too. I don't really get it but she reckons you put them on your phone somehow and then you can play all kinds of games or buy pizzas. Would you believe it? There's also something called Twitter. Joan says it's a social-media site, whatever that is. It even has its own special language to make it quicker to write. She taught me some of the words and what they mean:

LOL – Little Old Lady

JRME – Just Resting My Eyes

LMFAO – Left My Favourite Anorak Outside

NWDICIHF – Now What Did I Come In Here For?

OMG – Overcooked My Gammon

IENYK – I'm Eighty-Nine, You Know

GFAN – Gone For A Nap

ROFL – Rigid On the Floor, Leaking

She even helped me to set up an account: @Bridget89 (I've no idea what the eighty-nine means) but I changed it to @BridgetandJoan so we could do it together. She just looked at me and went all tearful again. She really is getting terribly sentimental in her old age, bless her.

## Sunday 7th

Another rainy day so Mrs Sharples insisted we 'make our own entertainment, just like in the old days'. We wanted to play poker but instead she introduced a game called 'If You Were a…' She said it was far more intellectually stimulating and encouraged lateral thinking. For example, I said if Bridget were a car, she would be a noisy little runaround. No class but a surprisingly accommodating interior.

And I said if Joan were a car, she'd be a hearse.

## Monday 8th

Much nicer day today. Spent the morning sitting on my favourite bench in the park, resting my eyes. I've sat on that bench more times than I care to remember. Perhaps when I'm gone they'll put a little plaque on it: 'In Loving Memory of Bridget Golightly who spent many a happy time sitting alone on this bench, and before that with her gentleman friends.'

Just had a look at Bridget's diary – purely in the spirit of friendship, of course. Honestly, a plaque on a park bench – who does she think she is? And if they're going to include all her gentleman friends, they're going to need a considerably longer bench.

## Tuesday 9th

Dolly Atherton went into hospital yesterday to have her bunions done and came out with breast implants. Whichever way you look at it, she still can't get her shoes on.

## Wednesday 10th

Mrs Sharples has finally acquiesced to my request. Sunday evening will see the First Second-Best Magnolia Retirement Home's Got Talent Talent Show (I've copyrighted the title in case anyone else tries to use it). The only question is, which of my many talents do I display? It would be unfair on the other contestants to use more than three or four. Oh well, I'd better tell Joan. Although goodness knows what she will do. Maybe that thing where she cracks her knuckles?

Just heard about Bridget's ridiculous scheme. Surprised she didn't call it the Bridget Show. She's in her room now, screeching something from *South Pacific* and dropping oranges. Hopefully, I'll catch pneumonia and won't be able to attend.

## Thursday 11th

I love doing crossword puzzles. Mrs Sharples says they really help keep your mind agile. I've just found a particularly difficult one – it's only made up of one-letter words. Now, where did I put my pen?

Just had to take Bridget's pen off her. She was writing on the chessboard again.

## Friday 12th

No luck on the pneumonia front, so I'm stuck watching this so-called talent show. I hope it doesn't go on too long, although with Bridget performing we'll probably still be here on Sunday.

## Sunday 14th

Thank heavens for that – finished at last. I think Bridget's strategy must have been to numb the judges into submission. It almost worked, too. Only two of the four are still breathing. All in all it was a varied line-up. Mr Cropper kicked it all off as the Amazing Memory Man (they say he can remember as far back as last November); Mr Gooch then gave us his energetic, if slightly obscene, OAP Diddy; Mrs Colstain and the Wilkinson triplets did their best as the Old Spice Girls; and Bridget 'treated' us to the full range of her talents, from tap dancing to sword swallowing to a marathon medley of every show tune ever written. Her grand finale was an uncanny and frankly disturbing take on Lady Gaga. She couldn't afford bacon so she wore a dress made from pork luncheon meat. Which didn't go down too well with the cook but went down rather too well with Mrs Fingall's dog act. Ever the trouper, Bridget continued undeterred, boldly declaring that 'The show must go on!' before disappearing beneath a pyramid of spaniels. And then just when I thought it was all over, Mrs Ferris was shot out of a cannon! She wasn't part of the show, it was just her last request. They'd mixed up her ashes with glitter to make a sparkling send-off (two parts glitter to one part Mrs Ferris).

I was robbed! How could I not have won? I gave them everything they wanted and so much more! I left nothing on that stage – apart from a few bits of pork luncheon meat. I even told them I was doing it for my dying nan. I can't believe Mrs Sharples gave that woman the first prize. And just for cracking her knuckles too.

## Monday 15th

Ever since Bridget got that damned iPhone, she keeps calling me all hours of the night.

11.24 p.m.

Me: 'Hello?'

B: 'Hello? Who is this speaking, please?'

Me: 'It's me. Joan. You called me, Bridget. What do you want?'

B: 'Oh hello, Joan. It's me, Bridget.'

Me: 'Yes, I know.'

B: 'Isn't this wonderful, Joan. Now we can talk as often as we like.'

Me: 'Yes. Wonderful.'

B: 'And it's so clear. It's like you're in the next room.'

Me: 'I am in the next room, Bridget.'

B: 'Oh yes, I forgot. Silly me. Only this telephone's so good it's as clear as if you were halfway round the world.'

Me: 'Goodnight, Bridget.'

B: 'Goodnight, Joan.'


1.18 a.m.

Me: 'Hello?'

B: 'Hello? Who is this speaking, please?'

Me: 'It's Joan again, Bridget. You called me. Again.'

B: 'Hello Joan. It's Bridget here.'

Me: 'What do you want, Bridget?'
B: 'Hello?'

3.27 a.m.

Me: 'Hello, Bridget.'
B: 'Hello, who is this speaking, please?'
Me: 'It's me, Bridget.'
B: 'Oh, is it? Then I must be Joan.'
Me: 'Goodnight, Joan.'
B: 'Goodnight, Bridget.'

The strangest thing. Joan's never shown any interest in my love life but suddenly, out of the blue, at half past three this morning, she suggested I try online dating. I told her I'd never been much good on skates but she said it was something on the Internet. She reckons they're all at it. And said she's sure they must have special sites for the more mature single – and me too. I told her I'd keep her updated on my progress but she said that could wait till morning and then the line went dead. I tried ringing her back several times but there was no reply – there must have been a fault on the line. So I shouted goodnight through the wall instead.

## Tuesday 16th

I must say, this Internet dating is terribly complicated. It's difficult to find the right site, there are so many to choose from. I looked at a few but they weren't at all what I was expecting – they certainly cater for all kinds.

Eventually, I came across one that looked perfect: Senior Moments: Dating for the Golden Generation. But when I looked through the members' profiles, I can't say I was all that impressed. They all looked so... well, old. Oh well, may as well give it a go, I suppose. If only to keep Joan happy. I made a note of a couple of the more exciting-sounding members...

Reginald

- Age: 82
- Hobbies: sitting, pottering in the garden, pottering in the house
- Favourite tipple: Ovaltine
- Favourite type of food: supper
- Dream destination: Cleethorpes
- I am looking for: companionship

Joe

- Age: 79
- Hobbies: sleeping on park benches
- Favourite tipple: white cider in a brown paper bag
- Favourite type of food: mashed up
- Dream destination: indoors somewhere
- I am looking for: a bed for the night

## Friday 19th

I'm glad I joined that Senior Moments dating site after all. I'm very popular – I've had five winks on my profile from gentlemen already!

Bridget was all excited about getting so many winks on that dating site. Turned out it was one old man with a nervous twitch.

## Saturday 20th

This iTelephone really is marvellous! It's jam-packed with ideas for places to go and things to do. We've been to a show every day this week – and they all had a free buffet afterwards!

Bridget's iPhone is a nightmare. We've been out every day since she found that 'Funerals Near U' app.

## Sunday 21st

Retirement-home quiz today. Bridget and I won. We were the only ones who could remember our names.

## Tuesday 23rd

7.02 p.m. Decided to skip Mrs Sharples's fascinating talk on bowel health for the over-seventies. Off out to the wrestling instead. I only hope Bridget doesn't spoil it for me. Professional wrestling is one of the few proper traditions left in this country. It's an art – a balletic combination of drama and athleticism. I like nothing better than to sit at the ringside in contemplative appreciation of the multitude of poetic moves and intricate combinations.

Seven o'clock. Joan's dragging me to the wrestling at the town hall this evening. It's not my kind of thing at all. I don't know what she sees in it – all that grunting and groaning and big sweaty masked men in skimpy, spangly undies, manhandling each other's privates. Hmmmm…

Eleven o'clock. Well, I have to say, that was a lot more fun than I'd expected! What with all that cheering and booing it was like being at the pantomime all over again. And Joan – I've never seen her so animated. The highlight of the evening was when the Towering Giganto challenged all-comers. I haven't seen Joan move so quickly since she last heard that her grandchildren were coming to visit. She would have beaten him too if she hadn't been disqualified for illegal use of a handbag. She may not have got his belt but at least she got his mask as a trophy. And I got his trunks. He didn't seem to mind, although that may have been the nitrous oxide the paramedics gave him on the way to the ambulance.

## Wednesday 24th

Went to the supermarket today. They had one of those new-fangled talking checkouts! It's amazing how lifelike they are.

Went to the supermarket today. Bridget kept chatting to the automated checkout. I had to hide and talk back to her or we'd still be there.

## Friday 26th

I'm still trying to decide what to make for Ivy Battle's 100th birthday present. At the moment it's a toss-up between an embroidered lavender bag or a cushion depicting her hysterectomy.

## Tuesday 30th

Definitely an umbrella day today. It's not raining, we just fancied poking a few people's eyes out as we walked down the high street.

# MAY

### Wednesday 1st

Had to wait ages to get into the bathroom this morning. Apparently Enid was in there having a bath with her toaster. Poor woman was in there for hours – she didn't know the power had been cut off because Mrs Sharples had spent the electric money on a new foot spa for her dog. Honestly, the way these power companies treat old people is terrible.

### Friday 3rd

Thought I'd go out for a little drive today to help myself relax. I shouldn't have bothered. It was so noisy. I came home soaked.

Bridget came home drenched again. How many times have I told her not to take her mobility scooter into the car wash?

### Monday 6th

It's so annoying taking Bridget out. She just sits there singing and shouting 'Are we there yet?' every five minutes. It annoys everyone else in the cinema too.

## Friday 10th

Given up on Senior Moments. It was a dead loss. Literally. Turned out most of the members passed away years ago. According to Mr Gooch, they just keep their profiles on there to fool lonely people into joining. Luckily, there's a speed-dating night at that new vodka bar in town tomorrow night. I haven't tried anything like that before but I'm willing to give it a go – I only hope they can keep up with me.

Have reluctantly agreed to take Bridget to some ghastly sounding dating event. On the strict understanding that my role is purely one of neutral observer.

## Saturday 11th

Managed to persuade Joan to accompany me to the speed dating. Just as well I did, as there were far more gentlemen than ladies there, not that I'm complaining! Anyway, after a little persuasion – and a lot of vodka – Joan took to it like a horse on fire. In fact, she ploughed her way through far more men than I did. Who knows, maybe there'll be a double wedding this year!

I can't believe I let Bridget talk me into joining in with this ridiculous charade. A bunch of grown women being herded around rows of tables full of desperate-looking retired men, being forced to talk to them for anything up to three minutes at a time. And on top of that, we had to make a list of the ones we'd seen and provide an assessment. This is mine:

1. Derek. Whistler
2. Bob. Mummy's boy
3. Clive. Drunk
4. Brian. Boring
5. Gerard. Welsh
6. Tom. Tiresome
7. Malcolm. Twitch
8. Tony. Spinach in teeth
9. Bruce. Teeth in spinach
10. Leonard. Asleep

What a fun evening – such a pity it was over so quickly. I barely had time to fill in the assessment form:

1. Nice gentleman. Very good listener. Could have talked to him all night. Don't think he told me his name. Or anything else, come to that…

There didn't seem to be time to talk to anyone else.

## Sunday 12th

Fancied a change from bingo tonight so I suggested to Joan that we try something different – like gender reassignment. Or eating at Nando's.

## Monday 13th

Must pop out to the mid-season sales. Apparently there are all sorts of bargains to snap up.

It doesn't matter what the time of year is, Bridget never misses the sales. She reckons she can shoplift twice as much for her money.

## Tuesday 14th

Despite her relentless grumpiness, I know that Joan has a good heart. That's why I'm sure we'll always be friends.

Despite her relentless cheerfulness, I know Bridget has a good heart. That's why I got her to fill out that organ-donor card.

## Wednesday 15th

Went to the park today and fed the ducks. We didn't intend to, only Bridget laid the picnic cloth down too close to the pond and, before we knew it, a rather cheeky mallard had snatched our sandwiches. I was all for letting bygones be bygones and heading for the cafe but Bridget was having none of it. Before you could say Johnny Weissmuller, she'd dived into the water and was embroiled in a death roll with the thieving bird. It was only when she went down for the third time that I remembered she couldn't swim. Luckily the pond was no more than four feet deep so I managed to wade out and drag her to the bank, getting my new hat and overcoat covered in pondweed in the process. And did she thank me? She just screamed and passed out, and I had to carry her all the way home too.

Oh dear, I've just had the most terrible nightmare! First I lost my sandwiches, then I was drowning in some huge lake. Somehow I managed to scramble my way out but as I was lying exhausted on the bank this huge swamp monster emerged from the lake and came straight for me. I screamed and I don't remember anything after that. Fair shook me up, it did. Must remember not to eat cheese sandwiches before I go to sleep again.

## Saturday 18th

Going out clubbing tonight. Popped a little bottle of vodka into my handbag to save money on drinks.

Bridget's going out clubbing tonight. Popped a little water into Bridget's vodka bottle. To save money on Alka-Seltzer.

## Wednesday 22nd

Bridget's had quite a few falls lately. Mrs Sharples is understandably concerned – she says it might reflect badly on the home – so she asked me to make a note of any incidents. She thinks Bridget may have an inner-ear condition whereas I suspect it's more of an in-the-pub condition.

Bridget's falls this month:

Down the stairs (twice)

Getting out of the bath

On the bus

Getting into the bath

In the shopping centre

Onto Father O'Brien

Into a bottle bank

## Monday 27th

Since the council gave us all these new different-coloured wheelie bins, it's getting much harder to keep up. Will it be the blue, green or brown one that Bridget falls into this week?

## Thursday 30th

Seven o'clock. It's Ivy Battle's 100th birthday tomorrow. She's going to be in all the newspapers, apparently. Can't think why – all she does is sit in the best chair in the lounge staring into space with her Yorkshire terrier, Munchkin, on her knee. Or asleep. It's very hard to tell the difference. What a waste of a top-of-the-range, three-speed, tilt-to-standing recliner with views of the Garden of Remembrance. Mrs Sharples is so terrified she'll pass away before the big day that she's been prodding the poor soul every half-hour since February.

7.10 p.m. Everyone seems very relieved that Ivy's going to make it to her 100th. Well, you've got to hand it to her, she's done very well to live this long on a pacemaker, half a liver and *The Best of Des O'Connor*.

## Friday 31st

Nine o'clock. It's all started. Mrs Sharples is running around like a headless chicken, the place is swarming with reporters and we've had to toast our own Pop-Tarts for breakfast. Everyone's asking about Ivy's secret to long life and what it's like to be the oldest tweeter in the world. I don't know what all the fuss is about – all she ever tweets is what she's had for tea, and that's really written by the care staff because she's long since lost all feeling in her hands. On the upside, exciting news! Everyone's going out to watch her fulfil her lifelong ambition this afternoon. A ride in a hot-air balloon! And she's made it very clear in her tweets that she wants to take both Munchkin and her very best friend Bridget with her. What a coincidence – that just happens to be one of my lifelong ambitions too! Some of the other residents were a little suspicious but what can I say? Tweets don't lie!

8.59 a.m. Mrs Sharples got poor old Ivy up at six this morning. She's been sitting there in her chair for hours, dribbling and stroking her little Munchkin. The reporters keep asking her the same thing. 'What's your secret for a long and happy life?' And each time she mumbles, 'No alcohol, no cigarettes and no men.' That's rich coming from a woman who spent most of the war drinking turps, smoking a pipe and charging half a crown for a bunk-up in her Morrison shelter. Bridget seems very excited about going on this 'once in a lifetime' ride with her 'best friend' Ivy. I dread to think how much she had to bribe the care staff to get the old dear's Twitter password.

One o'clock. Thank goodness all that messing about with the mayor is over and done with. Time for that hot-air balloon ride at last! I've got the job of holding Ivy's little Munchkin – lively little thing he is; spends half the time licking his bottom and the other half licking mine! Joan's sulking, of course. She said she was going to stay in her bedroom and do her jigsaw – she's clearly jealous of my friendship with Ivy. I managed to persuade her to come along in the end. To hold my handbag. And my coat. And my hat. And to tell the reporters my name and all about my glittering show-business career. Oh well, here we go...

3.12 p.m. What a fiasco. Never seen anything like it. Television crews, reporters and half the town's dignitaries waiting two hours in a field for old Ivy to hobble along the red carpet to the balloon. They finally managed to hoist her in, closely followed by Bridget, who had that hairy rat strapped to one arm like a glove puppet and was doing a royal wave with the other. Then, as the mayor stepped forward to untie the rope and the pilot prepared to climb in, disaster struck. Munchkin suddenly jumped out of the basket. Bridget made a valiant attempt to grab him but instead caught hold of the rope as she toppled out onto the unsuspecting pilot. Before anyone knew what was occurring, the balloon jolted upwards with poor Ivy peering over the top and clinging on for dear life, and disappeared into the wide blue yonder…

10.34 p.m. Still no sign of Ivy. There was a sighting of her balloon over a shopping centre near Glasgow. But it turned out to be an inflatable cheeseburger.

# JUNE

## Saturday 1st

A real red-letter day! It's not every day that you get a letter with red writing all over the envelope – very exciting! My fingers trembled as I tore it open, eager to see what was inside – maybe a lovely card or an invitation to a tea party at Buckingham Palace. Imagine my disappointment when I saw it was just full of ordinary sheets of paper covered in numbers. I couldn't make head nor tail of it so I let Joan have a look. Very odd – she went completely white. I asked her if it was some kind of secret message, but she didn't say a word. She just gave me one of her rolly-eyes looks and walked out of the room.

I can't believe it. Just read Bridget's credit-card bill. How on earth has she managed to rack up a debt of twenty thousand pounds? Must be all that online shopping and Texas hold 'em. I didn't know how to break it to her at first but then I decided it was best to follow the old maxim, 'Be cruel to be kind'. So I carefully explained the financial trouble she was in, and even gave her a Chinese burn to be extra kind.

## Monday 3rd

That's the last time I go with Bridget to the leisure centre! It was so embarrassing – I can't believe she weed in the swimming pool. And the badminton court. And the bus on the way home.

## Tuesday 4th

I'll never forget the coronation. I waved my Union Jack so patriotically that I caught the eye of Her Majesty! And a nice policeman.

I'll never forget the coronation. Bridget had nine brown ales and got arrested for throwing her Union Jack knickers at the queen.

## Wednesday 5th

Thank goodness. I've been so worried about that credit-card bill but I knew something would turn up. I was just watching Jeremy Kyle this morning when a commercial with a nice young blonde lady came on! Old-and-a-Loan, they're called. They've got five shops on the high street so I popped along right away. They were terribly friendly and ever so keen to help me out. They said they didn't normally give out such large sums to a first-timer but they would make an exception, and give me a huge amount of interest. Isn't that nice? Joan hardly shows any interest at all.

## Thursday 6th

Bridget and I were bored today so we went for one of our walks. One of the slow ones on a really narrow pavement. A new record – we managed to get twenty-six people stuck behind us.

## Friday 7th

Went to a lovely trendy coffee shop today. Had something called a cappuccino. Ended up with a chocolate moustache!

Went to an awful trendy coffee shop today. Spent ages trying to rub Bridget's chocolate moustache off. Turned out to be a real one.

## Sunday 9th

Lovely day at Dunston Abbey. Whenever we visit a stately home I like to imagine I'm the lady of the manor. I wander from room to room, soaking up the centuries until I almost believe I'm back there. I could have stayed all day.

Terrible day at Dunston Abbey. I finally persuade Bridget to go to a stately home and all she does is charge round the place like a rabbit on Ritalin to get to the gift shop as quickly as possible.

My purchases:

1. Two-thousand-page hardback history of Dunston Abbey, from the Tudors to the twenty-first century

Bridget's purchases:

1. Dunston Abbey pencil

2. Dunston Abbey pencil sharpener

3. Dunston Abbey pencil case (containing Dunston Abbey pencil and pencil sharpener)

4. Nodding Dunston the Dachshund

5. Dunston Abbey key ring

6. Dunston Abbey fridge magnet

7. Dunston Abbey mouse pad

8. Dunston the Dolphin beanie toy

9. Three bottles of Dunston Abbey sherry

10. Signed photograph of the cast of *Dunston Abbey* television series

11. Dunston the Dinosaur beanie hat

## Monday 10th

Finally confronted Bridget about her spending. She swore she couldn't remember any of it. Although I have little faith in her capacity for recall, as Mrs Sharples would call it, I gave her a little advice about the dangers of identity theft and suggested she buy a shredder. So far she's shredded her shoes, her photographs and her best cardigan.

## Tuesday 11th

I love this time of year – time to put those winter clothes into storage and unleash my summer wardrobe on the world!

Winter clothes to put away:

Blue cardigans – 6

Thick black sweaters – 5

Grey woolly jumpers – 8

Summer clothes to take out:

Pink cardigans – 6

Thick yellow sweaters – 5

Mauve woolly jumpers – 8

## Wednesday 12th

I love a nice quiet night in watching television. Sadly, it's not as entertaining as it used to be.

Finally found Bridget. She was sitting in the kitchen, staring at the microwave.

## Friday 14th

How thrilling, the fair's come to town! What a night. I must have gone on everything at least twice! The waltzers, the dodgems, the hook-a-duck. Good job Joan's got such long arms – I couldn't have carried that big cuddly Billy the Brontosaurus round all night by myself. I'm sure she had a lovely time too, waving at me every time I came round on the little carousel. And the giant centipede. And the medium-sized squid. The only thing I managed to persuade Joan to go on was the Ghost Train. She's definitely at her best in the dark. Of course, I had to hold her hand so she wasn't too frightened. She always puts a brave face on it but I know that deep down she's a quivering wreck.

What a night. Spent most of it carrying that daft dinosaur around. And the cuddly toy she won. Then I was forced to watch while she whooped, screamed and threw up on every ride they had. The only thing worth going on was the Ghost Train. Only problem was, Bridget wouldn't let go of me the whole way round. Every time a klaxon sounded or a cardboard skeleton flew out at us she gripped me so tightly that I thought my varicose veins were going to burst. She even jumped when we got to the end and the young man gave her a goldfish. He gave me one too. Apparently they had several left over after the rifle-range stallholder suddenly had to close shortly after Bridget had a go. Luckily the St John's Ambulance men had plenty of bandages and morphine.

## Saturday 15th

It's so relaxing watching our fish swimming round and round. Joan said I can't have them in my room as she doesn't think she can cope with the responsibility. She's never been very good with animals ever since she was a girl and she had to bury her pet dog, Buster. He wasn't dead, she just got bored with him. I must say, fish really do have individual personalities. The small one darts around like a mad thing while the bigger one just floats there looking miserable. I've been trying to think of names for them all day. Then suddenly they came to me: Bridget and Joan. I don't know why.

## Sunday 16th

Joan and I are doing our Saturday shop in Asda. And it looks like I've got an admirer! A lovely tall young gentleman keeps following me around, undressing me with his steely blue eyes. Poor Joan's quite envious. She always did like a man in uniform.

Bridget seemed desperate for that security guard to notice her, so I thought I'd help her out. I told him she's been putting tins of salmon in her coat pocket.

## Monday 17th

Goodness, it's so hot I've decided to sleep naked tonight!

When Bridget said she was going to sleep naked, I didn't think she meant in her armchair during *Emmerdale*.

## Wednesday 19th

Just checked my New Year's resolutions. Now, which should I try for this month? Hmmm… I've not managed to find the love of my life yet. I'd better pull my finger out or I'll have Alf and Irene on my back again. Maybe I should have another look on my computer. See if I can't find another one of those dating sites, one more suited to a woman in the prime of life. And with some men in the prime of theirs too. Or even just with any life.

## Thursday 20th

Four o'clock. Yippee! I've found the perfect dating site: ToyBoys'R'Us. Far more my cup of tea. Lots of nice, strapping young gentlemen with plenty of stamina – and all looking for the more mature lady. I just need to fill in my profile and think of a suitable username. Hmmm… Lady Bridget of Magnolia Hall has a nice ring to it.

Half past six. Right, I've put in my details, now I suppose I just wait. It's a good job I'm patient by nature. I'm sure it won't take long, though – I can't imagine they get too many people like me on there!

### Friday 21st

Waiting…

### Saturday 22nd

Waiting…

### Sunday 23rd

Still waiting…

### Monday 24th

Seven o'clock. Ooh, somebody's just sent me a wink! Whippersnapper 92 – looks a bit like that nice Justin Bieber. I think I might have to send him a wink back.

Five past seven. Ooh, he's got my wink and sent me a kiss! I'd better send him one back. Be rude not to…

Half past nine. Well, I'm quite exhausted! We've winked,

kissed, held hands, fondled, groped and, well, I'm not quite sure what that last picture was but it looked awfully uncomfortable. This is all going so fast…

## Thursday 27th

Half past seven. Getting very nervous about my first date with my toy boy at Café Olé this morning. I just need to nail down my look. Should I go Julie Andrews or Dita Von Teese? I don't want to appear too conservative but I don't want to risk inflaming that Italian barista's ardour again with my natural, overwhelming *je ne sais quoi*. Maybe I'll go down the middle and opt for Lady Gaga.

9.12 a.m. Bridget's getting in a right lather about this young gentleman she's supposed to be meeting – I don't know how many times she's changed her outfit. In the end, I must say I was pleasantly surprised by the classiness of her dress. Less so by the plastic lobster on her head. I've heard all sorts of tales about the type of men you meet on these Internet dates, so I suggested we set up an emergency phone-call system. If anything goes wrong, she's to ring 999.

Ten o'clock. Bit more nervous now. No sign of my date yet, so I'm killing time by sipping at my extra-grande cappuccino and writing in this diary, although it isn't easy, what with all the steam clouding my glasses. Joan doesn't normally let me have one of these – she says that all the caffeine only sends me giddy or rushing for the toilet.

Half past ten. Even more nervous now. Still no sign of him. On my second cappuccino. Not feeling remotely giddy or in need of the toilet – so much for Joan's medical opinion.

Eleven o'clock. Extremely nervous now. Maybe I shouldn't have had that third cappuccino. Maybe he isn't coming. Maybe I do need to go to the toilet after all…

Two o'clock. What a disaster! I used Joan's emergency system but who would have thought it would take the best part of three hours for the fire brigade to come and rescue me? I would have thought that the minute they heard my voice on the phone, they would have rushed to the scene, sirens blaring. And you would think that the lock on a disabled toilet would be on the inside, anyway! My toy boy must have thought I'd stood him up, the poor thing.

## Saturday 29th

Bridget was a bit glum after her date, in spite of all the firemen, so I suggested we watch the Glastonbury Festival on TV. Bridget loves the Rolling Stones – she's been training for months so that she can move like Jagger. Unfortunately, he now moves like Bridget.

# JULY

### Monday 1st

Noon. Hooray! I've found a job to help me pay off my loan. And I can do it from home too. And it will give me the opportunity to use my greatest skill: being a good listener. I'm working for a helpline – a bit like the Samaritans, I think. It's called Helping Hands. I found their card in the phone box. Vulnerable people ring me on my mobile phone. I can take all the calls in my room so I don't have to worry about Joan earwigging for once.

2.36 p.m. Earwigging? Me? Cheeky madam! Honestly, the things I read in Bridget's diary when I'm dusting it and it accidentally falls open. And I don't know what she means about being a good listener. Without her hearing aid she's as deaf as a post.

Midnight. What an evening. I've been on that phone all night! I've lost count of how many despairing souls I've saved. And my wrist is aching too – I have to log all the calls and keep the minutes. Good job I'm a fast writer…

8.15 p.m.

Me: 'Hello, dear, how can I help you?'

Caller: 'What are you wearing?'

Me: 'Me, dear? Why, my violet cardigan and a rather fetching pearl necklace, how about you, dearie?'

Caller: 'What?'

Me: 'What are you wearing?'

Caller (silence for forty-five seconds): 'Nothing…'

Me: 'Oh my goodness, you poor dear, you'll catch your death. I'll wait while you pop off and get something warm on.'

Caller: 'Listen, I've had a very stressful day and I just need you to help me, you know… finish myself off with your helping hands.'

Me: 'Oh, I don't think I'm supposed to do that, sweetie. I'm here to try and stop you doing anything silly like that.'

Caller: 'You are?'

Me: 'Yes, dearie.'

Caller: 'Are you sure?'

Me: 'Quite sure, dear.'

Caller: 'Oh. Er, could you at least… tell me I'm a naughty boy?'

Me: 'Are you a naughty boy?'

Caller: 'A… bit. I suppose.'

Me: 'Oh dear, that sounds awfully negative. I think I'm supposed to say you're a good boy.'

Caller: 'Oh. All right, then. Do good boys get spanked?'

Me: 'Of course not, dear. Good boys get a toffee!'

Caller hung up at 8.17 p.m.

## Tuesday 2nd

Just had a call from the helpline boss. He said they're going to have to let me go. Can't figure out what I did wrong. He reckoned I wasn't giving the callers what they needed but I thought I was very sympathetic. Even to that funny gentleman who was having trouble with his big throbbing clock. Oh well, back to the drawing board.

## Saturday 6th

It's so hot today. Joan's only wearing one jumper! And two cardigans. And her big coat. And gloves…

## Tuesday 9th

Mrs Sharples keeps telling Bridget off for chatting to that young pool cleaner with no top. Finally, Bridget's admitted she's right and gone to put one on.

## Wednesday 10th

Bridget had a near-death experience today. Her ninetieth birthday. (Not her sixty-sixth, as she keeps telling everyone.) She's been dropping subtle hints for weeks – whistling 'Happy Birthday' during breakfast, casually chatting about things she's always wanted and walking round the home carrying a placard with 'It's nearly my birthday!' painted on it. As usual she's arranged everything herself. Jelly and ice cream, a bouncy castle and a stripogram. All at once. I got her a cake with ninety candles, a card with a big ninety badge on it and a bottle of ninety-year-old sherry. Even Mrs Sharples got her a balloon with ninety on it. Then popped it behind her back.

## Friday 12th

Getting awfully excited about this year's holiday at the Costa Bella Sea View Hotel! I'm not sure exactly which part of Spain it's situated in – the name of the town's a little difficult to pronounce – but it sounds very exotic!

Bridget's getting awfully excited about this holiday. I can't imagine why, it's only Llandudno – same as last year. And the year before. And the year before that… Mind you, she knocks back so much sherry when she's away, it's not surprising she can't remember anything.

Half past eleven. Too excited to sleep, so I thought I'd make an early start and put my case by the front door so I don't keep the coach waiting in the morning.

11.32 p.m. Too thirsty to sleep. Went downstairs for a glass of water. Almost fell over Bridget in the hall. Wide awake, she was, all done up in her best bikini and sun hat, sitting on her case in the dark with her little legs dangling. When I turned the light on, she said, 'Are we there yet?' Turned it off again and went back to bed.

## Saturday 13th

11.14 p.m. What a start to the holiday. After twelve hours of listening to Bridget's snoring, we finally arrived at

Llandudno in the pitch dark and a force-ten gale. There was no sign of our hotel anywhere, so Mrs Sharples went to investigate. She returned half an hour later to announce that, unfortunately, we would no longer be staying at the Costa Bella Sea View Hotel on account of its no longer having a sea view. In fact it now has a cliff view, having been unexpectedly blown into the sea during *Antiques Roadshow*. But we weren't to worry because she'd 'performed miracles' and found a 'superb family-run establishment' nearby which, by lucky coincidence, just happened to be completely empty. It all sounded a bit fishy to me. Although not as fishy as the Costa Bella Sea View Hotel.

Half past eleven. What a lovely sleep! I woke just as the coach arrived at the hotel, refreshed and ready for anything. It was a bit rainy, but I'm sure it will have blown over by tomorrow – this Mediterranean weather can change so quickly. Joan was a little on the grumpy side but that's nothing new. I must say, it looks like a wonderful hotel. Very nice, attentive young man on reception. Didn't catch his name. Impeccable English. Couldn't take his eyes off me, said I reminded him of his mother. In her younger days, clearly. Joan seemed to perk up a bit when he suggested she and I share a room. The best in the hotel apparently, right next to his office. Well, I'd better get my beauty sleep, looks like a fun-packed week ahead!

11.36 p.m. What a dump. The Bates Family Hotel and Spa? Not sure where the spa is but the rooms are damp enough – no good at all for my chest. And there's something very peculiar about that manager, if you ask me. He couldn't take his eyes off Bridget. I say eyes – only one was actually fixed on her, the other seemed to be wandering about entirely of its own accord. And as if things weren't bad enough, they don't have sufficient rooms for us all, so Bridget and I are forced to share. I tried to object but I was too busy coughing at the time. Apparently, he's stuck us in his mother's old room. Or shrine, I should say, considering the giant portrait hanging over the mantelpiece. He's kept everything exactly the way it was when she was alive. Her clothes still hang in the wardrobe, her wig still sits on a polystyrene head on the dressing table, and her teeth are still floating in a glass by the bed. I'd better have a quick check under the duvet before we get in, just in case.

## Sunday 14th

10.13 a.m. Just seen today's programme of events. Looks dreadful:

- 10.30 a.m. Prayers in the local chapel
- 12.00 p.m. Carvery in the village pub, with a choice of three meats: roast lamb, braised lamb and mutton
- 3.00 p.m. Concert by the local male-voice choir
- 6.00 p.m. Dinner, consisting of bara brith, Welsh rarebit and leeks
- 7.00 p.m. Welsh bingo
- 8.00 p.m. Groovy Geraint and his sounds of the seventies

Quarter past ten. Just seen today's programme of events. Looks like we're not in Spain after all. Better tell Joan – hope she's not too disappointed.

## Monday 15th

Nine o'clock. Norman winked at me at breakfast! Unless it was a twitch – he is a bit twitchy. It's almost as if he's running the whole place on his own. Anyway, it's the highlight of the holiday for me today: swimming with dolphins! I'll be able to tick something else off my list. I wonder if it will get rid of my bad hip?

12.15 p.m. Bridget's wondering if swimming with dolphins will have any therapeutic effect. I told her that if she really wants to get rid of her bad hip, she should try swimming with sharks.

Four o'clock. So disappointed. They weren't real dolphins at all, just inflatable ones in the hotel pool. I had a go anyway, but it wasn't the same. I never felt we really bonded. Oh well, according to the noticeboard, we're being entertained by Tom Jones tonight! Maybe he'll do wonders for my hip instead…

6.32 p.m. Mrs Babbage, Miss Temple, Mrs Fayed and Miss Silverman have brought their violins and cellos with them and they're going to entertain us during dinner, and they've promised a full recital on Thursday evening. A bit of culture at last. Not that Bridget would notice – she's far too busy picking out a spare pair of big pants to throw at Tom Jones. Or possibly kidnap him in. Still can't believe he's actually performing in this dump. I suppose the credit crunch has hit us all.

10.49 p.m. Bridget needn't have bothered with the pants. It wasn't Tom Jones at all but a tribute act. To be fair, Mr Bates managed quite a jaunty opening with 'It's Not Unusual', then livened things up with 'Sex Bomb', gyrating his groin to full effect. I was slightly perturbed when he disrobed during 'You Can Leave Your Hat On' but Bridget didn't seem too concerned, of course. Things got a little tense when she giggled during his rendition of 'Delilah' and he rounded on her dramatically with the line 'I felt the knife in my hand and she laughed no more'. You could have cut the atmosphere with, well, a knife. Things seemed to calm down again as he sang his finale, 'The Green, Green Grass of Home', but when he fell to his knees at the end and screamed 'I'm doing this for you, Mother!' I made a mental note to double lock our bedroom door tonight. And push the chest of drawers in front of it.

3.29 a.m. Still can't sleep. Swear I saw Mr Bates's mother's eyes move. Well, one of them at least.

## Tuesday 16th

Nine o'clock. I'm sure Norman's twitch has got worse. I suppose trying to run a hotel when your mother's just died isn't all it's cracked up to be. Oh well, I expect he should be in his element this evening. Apparently, he's going to entertain us all with his stand-up comedy. Is there nothing that man can't do?

9.10 a.m. That vein is bulging in Mr Bates's temple again. Lord knows how he'll get through tonight's so-called comedy spectacular. Is there nothing that man can do?

Half past five. Had a lovely afternoon. We visited the pier and had a smashing fish lunch. Must say, my feet are aching a bit, though. I think I'll have a nice hot bath before the evening's entertainment.

5.27 p.m. Had a lovely afternoon. Managed to avoid the group outing to the pier and spent a nice relaxing time in our room, doing my crosswords – at least, it was relaxing when I turned that dreadful portrait round to face the wall.

And just when I thought the day couldn't get any better, Bridget told me she was going for a nice long bath when she returned. Maybe there is a God after all.

Seven o'clock. Oh my giddy aunt, I'm all of a fluster! Joan's getting me a stiff drink. I was just relaxing in the bath, soothing my aching feet, when I thought I'd pull the shower curtain round me and turn the light off for a little snooze. All of a sudden I heard the most terrifying music, and the shadow of a woman with an enormous knife appeared at the curtain! Then a pale, bony hand started to pull it back. I can't remember anything else. Oh dear, oh dear…

7.05 p.m. I knew it couldn't last. I was just filling in fifteen across and listening to Mrs Babbage's string quartet tuning up when I heard the most blood-curdling scream. Of course it was Bridget. My first thought was that she'd seen a spider in the bath. Or herself in the mirror. But apparently she'd pulled the emergency alarm cord thinking it was for the light. Mr Bates, all done up as his 'hilarious' comedy alter ego, Naughty Norma, rushed in, curling tongs in hand, to give her assistance but by the time he'd pulled aside the shower curtain, she'd fainted clean away. He was so distraught that he cancelled tonight's show, so every cloud has a silver lining. Although he did insist on turning his mother's portrait round again. And making me apologise to her for turning it round in the first place. The sooner we're out of this place, the better…

## Wednesday 17th

Ten o'clock. I do feel silly now that Joan's explained last night's little mix-up. Thought I'd better go and apologise to Norman. He was very understanding. In fact, we had a nice long chat. It turns out he always wanted to be an entertainer but was forced to spend his life looking after his mother and her hotel. I couldn't help feeling sorry for the poor man. 'Don't be depressed,' I said. 'Not everyone can be a West End star.' 'I didn't want to be a West End star,' he replied, 'I wanted to be a Butlins Redcoat!' Tragic.

Oh well, at least he's got the chance to wow us all with his magic show tonight. I'll be wearing my lowest-cut cardigan especially for him too. I know he's not feeling his best at the moment but I've got a strange feeling what he really wants is an older woman. Not sure why.

11.10 p.m. Just when I thought we'd seen everything that our beloved host had to offer, he sprang out from behind the dining-room curtain in a big hat. Yet another alter ego: 'internationally acclaimed' magician, the Great Orme. Everything went surprisingly well to begin with. He drew a string of handkerchiefs from his pocket, an egg from his mouth and even a live rabbit from his hat. But then it was time for his big finale: sawing the lady in half. 'Any volunteers?' he shouted dramatically, whipping his electric carving knife from his coat pocket. Not surprisingly, given the previous six days, volunteers were a little thin on the ground. Even Bridget was unusually subdued, although that may have been the sherry. After numerous further requests, he became increasingly frustrated and began pointing his knife at guest after guest, jabbering, 'Oh go on, let me saw you in half. It's perfectly safe – I've got a certificate.' His patter became even more alarming as the audience cowered from his blade. 'Come on, ladies, what's the worst that could happen? After all, how much longer have you got left, anyway?' In the end he resorted to running up and down the dining room, rabbit clinging to his head for dear life, jabbing out at any protruding limb. You should have heard the screams, it was quite a show! And, as a bonus, we all get to go home early as the hotel has been closed down and Mr Bates has been sectioned. Now that's what I call entertainment.

Midnight. Well, Norman was magnificent as ever tonight. I can't say I completely understood his act – I imagine it was some kind of Welsh interpretive dance – but it was certainly very impressive, from the wild staring eyes to the fake blood everywhere and his plaintive cry of 'Mother, why are you making me do this?' at the end. The only disappointment was that I was hoping to waylay him after the show. I waited several minutes outside his office but then Joan turned up to tell me he'd had to leave suddenly because he'd been sectioned. Isn't it amazing what you can do with those modern electric carving knives?

## Friday 19th

Schools broke up for the summer today. No sooner had we stepped off the bus than this little devil on his skateboard almost sent us flying. Then the cheeky monkey stopped to give us a load of abuse! I had the shakes and Joan had one of her funny turns – the one where she twists round suddenly and ends up kicking him in the face. As she says, that black belt's not just for keeping her knickers up.

## Wednesday 24th

Scorching hot day. I've decided to be daring and sunbathe in the nude – there's nothing quite like the feeling of sand between your buttocks!

Sweltering hot day. I think I'd better take Bridget home – she's scaring the children in the sandpit!

## Friday 26th

Goodness, with everything that's been going on, I completely forgot to check ToyBoys'R'Us. Couldn't believe how many winks were sitting there waiting for me. Looks like there are plenty more fish in the sea – or dogs in the park, in this case: Young Pup 91. He says he'll be on the common around two o'clock on Wednesday afternoon, walking his chihuahua, and would I like to join him. No problem choosing what to wear this time – my all-weather, hand-crocheted poncho! And I even know where I can get a dog...

So, Bridget's off on another wild goose chase. Or wild dog chase, I should say. I was a little concerned when she said she was off to the common for a spot of dogging but when she carried on, I realised what she meant. I felt I should put her right on her terminology – but where's the fun in that?

## Wednesday 31st

Another disappointment! It was a lovely sunny afternoon on the common. I arrived bang on two with dog in tow. I can't imagine Mrs Sharples would have minded me borrowing her Hannibal for a few hours. I'm sure I read somewhere that Rottweiler/Doberman crosses need plenty of exercise. But I was in for a surprise. When I got there the place was teeming with lovely young gentlemen, all walking chihuahuas! I couldn't see my Young Pup anywhere but then I remembered what Joan said about people on dating sites not always using their real photographs. Of course, I don't approve of such deception myself but I thought it would be a good idea to keep an open mind. I didn't want to risk missing him, so I decided it was best to approach each and every young man until I found my cheeky young scamp. Sadly, I had no luck. None of them was my toy boy. Some even ran away when I suggested we go dogging in the nearby woods.

Then it occurred to me – and I made straight for my favourite park bench, the one that's been so good to me over the years. And lo and behold, there he was, chihuahua by his side. We had a lovely chat, although he was a little quiet. Even our dogs seemed to get on well.

In fact, I had trouble separating the two of them when I finally went. And to make things even better, just as I was leaving the common, a nice young uniformed gentleman suddenly turned up and offered to accompany me back to his place.

I wonder where Bridget can have got to? I hope she isn't still at the common. According to the headlines in the *Evening Herald*, there was all sorts going off there earlier. DEVIL DOG EATS CHIHUAHUA and PONCHO PERVERT ARRESTED FOR BECKONING YOUNG MEN INTO WOODS.

# AUGUST

### Thursday 1st

After all that to-do yesterday, I've decided to stay indoors for a few days and catch up on a bit of television. The desk sergeant thought that might be a good idea too. I do like that Dragon programme, especially that cheery Duncan Valentine. It's amazing the crazy ideas people come up with to earn a few bob. Then I came up with one of my own – Zimmertising! It's so obvious I can't believe no one's done it before. All I have to do is get local businesses to pay to have their services displayed on an advert attached to the front of a Zimmer frame. We've got twenty potential walking advertising hoardings in this home alone. I'll be a millionaire!

Bridget told me about her new money-making scheme. I hated to burst her bubble, but I had to point out its one slight flaw – it's utterly ridiculous. I'm sure she won't be deterred though – after all, the mark of a successful entrepreneur is an unfailing determination never to give up in the face of adversity.

## Friday 2nd

I give up in the face of adversity! Joan clearly doesn't think the world is ready for my outside-the-box innovations. I'll just have to adopt a more prosaic strategy in my struggle to clear my debts. Sit here and pray for a miracle.

## Monday 5th

They say a cup of tea's best when you've had a shock. So before Joan drinks hers, I always jump out of her wardrobe and shout 'Boo!'

Must get a lock for that wardrobe door. And a new cardigan.

## Friday 9th

Took Bridget to the doctor's with her skin today. He told her to stop picking at it and gave her some ointment. And one of those cones dogs wear.

## Tuesday 13th

Would you believe it? I've just won an all-expenses-paid mini-break for two to London next weekend, courtesy of GreyDays Travel, including a thousand-pound gift voucher!

It was one of those phone-in competitions on *Brenda and Alan's Just Our Cup of Tea*. The only problem is, who do I take? With all these toy boys chasing me, I'm bound to disappoint someone.

Bridget just asked me if I'd like to go with her to London for the weekend. Apparently she won a competition on some dreadful daytime TV show. All she had to do was answer one multiple-choice question: who is the current prime minister? She got it right on the third go. I'm disappointed she didn't choose someone else – I was hoping to make significant inroads into my jigsaw this weekend. Oh well, I'd better make the most of it, I suppose. It might be an opportunity to introduce Bridget to a bit of culture for once.

Places to visit in London:

The British Museum (to disprove Bridget's theory that we evolved from guinea pigs)

Highgate Cemetery (to pay our respects to the great Karl Marx)

The National Gallery (to show Bridget there's more to art than tattoos. I've told her often enough not to waste her money; I can always join up her varicose veins with a permanent marker)

The Royal Observatory (to prove to Bridget that she's not the most important thing in the universe)

Churchill War Rooms (to clarify once and for all to Bridget the difference between our wartime leader and a talking dog in an insurance commercial)

The Globe Theatre (to expose Bridget to the work of our greatest writer)

The Royal Opera House (to introduce Bridget to real music)

The British Library (to show Bridget what a book looks like)

Places to visit in London:

Harrods (to introduce Joan to the concept of opening her purse)

The London Eye (so that I can be higher than Joan for once)

London Zoo (to show Joan the guinea-pig enclosure)

Notting Hill (to find the bookshop that nice Hugh Grant works in, let him hide me from the paparazzi, fall in love with me and marry me. Can skip the bit about reading the book on a garden bench if we're short of time)

Camden Market (hoping to pick up one of those lovely talking dogs from the insurance commercial)

Soho (to expose Joan to a more colourful cultural experience)

Madame Tussauds (to pay our respects to the great Cliff Richard)

West End theatre (Joan says she'd love to see something postmodern or Brechtian. She's in for a treat – I've got tickets for *Huey Lewis and the News: The Musical*!)

## Wednesday 14th

Lovely day. I ran into an old friend I hadn't seen for years. You should have seen the look on her face!

Terrible day. Bridget lost control of her mobility scooter and careered into a bus queue. Luckily she only ran over one of them.

## Friday 16th

11.38 a.m. So much for this trip being all expenses paid. I had to buy my own train ticket. As usual, Bridget got away without having to pay – she jumped the barriers at the station. I say jumped, more pretended to faint so that someone carried her through (although I'm not sure he was entirely convinced that she was pregnant). Of course, then she had to spend the entire journey in the toilet. The guard wasn't suspicious as she always does that anyway. To make matters worse, the train was delayed for an hour while they forcibly removed Enid from the line.

Three o'clock. In our lovely hotel room at last! Unfortunately, the lift wasn't working so we had to walk up the stairs. Of course, being an ex-Olympian, I sailed up them in no time. Just waiting for Joan – it's taking her a little longer as she's not in such good shape as me. Anyway, at least it gives me time to take in the view.

3.11 p.m. Finally in our hotel room. When we arrived, the bellboy kindly took Bridget's cases. And gave them to me. Bridget keeps banging on about the view. It ought to be good, we're on the eighteenth floor!

## Saturday 17th

12.26 p.m. Exhausting morning in Harrods. They say you can buy everything there. Unfortunately, Bridget seemed to think this was an instruction. She dragged me round every square foot of shop floor space, stacking box on top of box in my arms like I was her personal shopper. I had half a mind to tell her where she could stick her parrot's head umbrella but unfortunately it was already stuck in my mouth.

Half past twelve. Amazing morning in Harrods. I felt like royalty with my prize gift voucher. The assistants couldn't do enough for me. If only the same could be said of Joan. You should have heard her griping just because I asked her to hold a couple of things for me. Unfortunately, when we got to the taxi, there wasn't enough room for my few little items of shopping and Joan, so she had to go on one of those lovely Boris bikes. I gave her my spare blonde wig so that she looked the part. In fact, the likeness was uncanny...

5.36 p.m. Went for a picnic in Hyde Park. Bridget was so excited to see the giant Colin Firth statue, she almost had a stroke. But she couldn't quite reach.

## Sunday 18th

Half past four. What a lovely afternoon at London Zoo. I haven't been since 1930-something. If I recall rightly, Joan was with me then too. Of course we were both little girls at that time. Well, I was at least – Joan's always had a more substantial build. I think if she and I were in a zoo, I'd have to be something cute and perky like a meerkat. And Joan would be Guy the gorilla.

4.39 p.m. London Zoo was even worse than the last time we came, all those years back – if that's possible. At least Bridget didn't lock me in the monkey house this time. I think if Bridget and I were in a zoo, she'd have to be something intensely irritating like a meerkat. And I'd be her keeper.

Quarter to five. It was so wonderful to be so close to all those beautiful creatures in their lovely homes. Especially the chimpanzees – they look just like little hairy people. In fact, I think one of them took a bit of a shine to me. He even gave me a present. I guess my legendary poise and elegance are irresistible to all species.

4.45 p.m. It was so sad to see all those beautiful creatures away from their natural environment. The only enjoyable part of the afternoon was when that adult male chimp flung its faeces at Bridget. I'm not an expert on animal expressions but I think he looked quite surprised when she returned the compliment.

## Monday 19th

Two o'clock. Heading home on the train. Goodness, what a mad whirl. They say when you're bored with London, you're bored with life. That's certainly true! We were so busy having fun, I only had time to record a few bits in my diary!

2.06 p.m. Heading home at last. Bored with London, bored with life.

Review of London trip:

The British Museum (time in museum: eight minutes. Time in gift shop: forty-five minutes)

The National Gallery (amazing. Wherever Bridget went, the security guards' eyes seemed to follow her round the room. We were finally asked to leave when Bridget tried to join up the dots on Georges Seurat's *Bathers at Asnières*)

The Royal Observatory (ejected when Bridget complained that a place dedicated to heavenly bodies should include hers)

Churchill War Rooms (thrown out when Bridget persisted in growling 'Oh yes, yes, yes')

The Globe Theatre (removed after Bridget paid excessive attention to young male tour guide's codpiece)

The Royal Opera House (asked to leave when Bridget insisted on singing ''Ave a banana' after every verse)

The British Library (left in ambulance after Bridget was crushed beneath the large-print edition of *War and Peace* while trying to reach for *Fifty Shades of Grey*)

## Wednesday 21st

Must hide my sherry better – just found Bridget throwing bread into the lavatory. She said she was feeding the toilet ducks.

## Thursday 22nd

What a stroke of luck! I knew something would come up. There I was just walking down the high street, minding my own business, when this nice young man comes up to me out of nowhere and asks me if I've ever been in the movies. I thought, I know your game, young man – you're just trying to get into my big pants. Unfortunately, it turned out he was serious. He said he was the managing director of Silver Screen Idols, a talent agency for the over sixties. He gave me this form to fill in and told me to pop round to his office on Friday to take some screen shots and a little video for him to send out to television companies and advertising agencies. How exciting! The last time I was on the television I was Dead Woman on Trolley Number Two in *Holby City*. At least until I had my sneezing fit.

Don't know what Bridget's up to now but I found this form while I was doing my weekly tidy of her room.

Name: Bridget LaFontaine

Age: mind your own business

Facial type: a young Judi Dench

Figure: a shorter, slimmer Cyd Charisse

Acting experience: Dame Maggie Smith's stunt double in *The Prime of Miss Jean Brodie*; also appeared in a number of tasteful silent artistic films

Singing experience: voiced Audrey Hepburn in *My Fair Lady*, Julie Andrews in *The Sound of Music*, Judy Garland in *The Wizard of Oz* and Baloo the bear in *The Jungle Book* (during bout of bronchitis)

Languages: English, French, love

Other talents: horse riding, tightrope walking, a little thing with ping-pong balls I picked up in Thailand

So that's it, she must be desperate. She always said she would never act again. That's if she ever did in the first place. I know we lost touch for a while and she claims she was in all sorts of films and shows but the only thing I remember was that amateur-dramatic production of *Sweeney Todd* just after we left school. As I recall, she was the third syphilitic prostitute from the left. I forget what part she played. Sadly, Bridget never gets offered such romantic roles any more – the acting brain may still be sharp but the old lady parts have long since dried up.

## Friday 23rd

Nine o'clock. So excited! I sent off my form and my enrolment fee and this morning I'm off to the office to get my publicity shots. I never imagined for one moment that I would be on television again. It must have been in the stars!

Noon. Well, that's most peculiar. I don't understand. I'm sure I got the address right. 38 Calloway Street. I looked and looked but Calloway Street only goes up to number 36. I tried there just in case but the man said they hadn't heard of any Silver Screen Idols talent agency. Although they did say I was the third old woman who had asked them this morning. Old! Blooming cheek – I'm in my prime, I am!

I was still trying to figure out what could have happened when, just as I was turning into our road, I bumped into Mrs Willows from the day centre. What a coincidence: she was carrying a form just like mine. I asked where she'd got it and she said this nice young man had given it to her. He said she had the most incandescent skin and an allure only found on the silver screen. Well, I knew something wasn't right. No one could describe Mrs Willows's skin as incandescent. And she's about as alluring as Mrs Potter's rice pudding. And then I got it.

12.10 p.m. Bit worried about Bridget. She hasn't been in to interrupt my jumbo crossword for hours. Maybe she's sickening for something. I'd better go and check in on her. Soon as I've finished seventeen down.

Three o'clock. Dear diary, that man at number thirty-six was right. I am an old woman. A silly, stupid old woman. As if anyone would think I should be on the television. I must have been mad. And I sent him the last of my savings, too. I should've known better at my age. When will I learn?

## Saturday 24th

Just thought I'd give that dating site one last chance. And aren't I glad I did! There he was, winking furiously at me: Texas Toy Boy! Quite dishy, got a look of a young George Clooney about him. Joan will be so envious – I must tell her.

## Sunday 25th

Woken up by Bridget. Bit of a lie-in for once, it was only half past five. She was all of a flap. Couldn't make head nor tail of what she was saying. Something about George Clooney, I think. Told her to have a cold shower and go back to bed.

## Tuesday 27th

Just had an email from my Texas Toy Boy and he really is from Texas. He says he can't believe someone hasn't already snapped me up. I said I couldn't believe it either but there's no accounting for taste. He's called Charles 'Chuck' Dubois the Third. I do like Americans, they're so charming and full of life!

Bridget's just come bounding into my room again. She's obviously feeling much better. Says she's found some new young stud on the Internet. Doesn't seem to know much about him, except he's some kind of flash executive – very prominent in boxer shorts, apparently. And he's American. Can't stand Americans.

## Wednesday 28th

Felt on top of the world when I woke up this morning, so I gave myself a splash of Chanel No. 5 and put on my new lime-green grankini before I went out.

I don't think I'll ever forget the sight of Bridget in her grankini. Nor will Father O'Brien or the rest of the congregation.

# SEPTEMBER

## Sunday 1st

Very satisfied with jigsaw progress over the last few weeks. Ever since Bridget's been corresponding with this Texan toddler, there seem to be so many more hours in the day. And quiet ones too.

## Wednesday 4th

Lovely trip to the supermarket. It was so magical – sparkly garlands and enormous baubles hanging from the ceiling, fairy lights on the tills, shelves crammed with tins of chocolates, selection boxes and Christmas puddings. Even the security guard was dressed as Santa and doing a little dance. I do love it when the Christmas season finally starts to lift the post-holidays gloom. I took the opportunity to buy Joan's Christmas card, just in case I forget. She'd never forgive me – she practically lives for Christmas. Poor dear, she hasn't got much else to look forward to.

Flabbergasting trip to the supermarket. I can't believe it! I only went there to get some plant food and the entire gardening section had been replaced by Christmas cards and decorations, if you please. September? I've barely dried my summer cardigans and put them away. They'd got some bearded animatronic monstrosity at the entrance that jiggled about and went 'Ho, ho, ho!' every time you went within five yards of it. I had to drag Bridget away or she'd still be flirting with it now. She loves Christmas, of course; she's been singing 'Here Comes Santa Claus' for a month already and spending even more money she hasn't got. I notice she bought me another card – that's three already. I think last year's total was nine.

## Saturday 7th

Off out to the annual Knitting Circle's dinner dance. Although I hate to leave Chuck on his own at the keyboard all evening. (I can't imagine there's much else on the Internet to keep young men entertained.) There's a free raffle tonight – that's why I'm wearing my lucky pants!

Just heard the dinner dance is providing free drinks all night, so I've reminded Bridget to wear her lucky pants. The ones with the rubber lining.

## Sunday 8th

Had a smashing time at bingo tonight!

Winning lines – 5

Full House – 2

Winnings – £5

Pleasure I gave with my singing – priceless

Had a terrible time watching Bridget have a smashing time at bingo tonight.

Winning lines – zero (couldn't hear numbers for Bridget's singing)

Winnings – zero

False calls from Bridget – 21

Times I had to stab Bridget with my bingo dabber – lost count

## Tuesday 10th

Thank goodness Mrs Sharples has banned Bridget from using the Internet. The queue for the computer was longer than the queue for the bathroom. Finally I can check how my fantasy-football team is getting on. Last time I looked, Gordon Banks had let in a first-half hat-trick.

Woe is me! Star-crossed lovers mercilessly torn asunder by a cruel twist of fate and Mrs Sharples's new rota system. What am I to do? Bad enough to be separated by a tempestuous ocean, but now we are denied even words and our continent-spanning romance is doomed to shrivel and die like a delicate rose without sunlight. Oh, he's just texted me.

## Thursday 12th

It takes so long to walk down the high street these days, what with all those charity collectors everywhere you look. They try to get away but Bridget won't let them.

## Tuesday 17th

Apparently, Enid's getting increasingly despondent about her failed suicide attempts so she's decided not to take any chances – she's going on hunger strike. Unfortunately it's her favourite today – gammon – so she's going to start tomorrow.

## Thursday 19th

Oh, for goodness' sake, Bridget's driving me to distraction! Doesn't matter where she is – in the TV room, at the dining table, on the toilet – all I hear is her little thumbs bashing away. The Lord alone knows how much it must be costing her, sending that many texts. I would have thought this silliness would have fizzled out a long time ago. Still, I'm sure it's only a matter of time. What with him being in America, and her being in her own little world.

## Saturday 21st

8.59 a.m. Looking forward to the village fete today. It's got everything a good old-fashioned fete should have: the Women's Institute tea tent, a steam engine, ferret racing, archery, a walking-stick demonstration and, of course, the annual pig-agility trials, 'One Man and His Hog'.

Nine o'clock. Looking forward to the village fete today! There'll be everything a good old-fashioned fete should have: a beer tent full of rugby players, eye candy galore with the local fire brigade and police sniffer-dog handlers, lovely sweaty blacksmiths and, of course, that gorgeous Barry Cook is judging the baking competition this year!

10.57 a.m. We've got here nice and early, I want to make sure my sultana-and-cinnamon buns (my mother's recipe) are delivered safe and sound before Bridget can destroy them. They're a particularly good batch so I'm expecting them to win Gold in the Baked Teatime Goods category, same as the last thirty years. Bridget's been talking about entering her famous cheese-and-herb scones but, as I reminded her, she's been barred from the competition since 2003, when she was disqualified for putting a banned substance in her Victoria sponge. She nearly got away with it, but someone was suspicious and demanded a test, which came back positive for Viagra. Nobody could deny it was well risen. As were the men who sampled it.

Eleven o'clock. Joan's being terribly smug about her buns. They're like her in many ways – flat, dry and not fruity enough – but no doubt she thinks she's going to win again. I'm sure she's got something over those judges – I'm still suspicious it was her that demanded a drugs test on my Victoria sponge. Anyway, I'll wipe the smile off her face with my cheese-and-herb scones. I don't know what it is about those plants I bought from that nice man with the dreadlocks at the car-boot sale the other week, but ever since I added them to my recipe, the residents can't get enough of them. You should see them grin and snigger after they've had a few. What a gift to be able to spread such happiness with your food! I may have been barred from the competition but I'm entering under a false name anyway. I don't know, using banned substances in my baking? As if anyone would be so potty...

2.17 p.m. Oh dear, Bridget's had three pints of real ale already. She's making a terrible fool of herself, flirting with half the beer tent. And the fire brigade. And the police dog handlers. And the police dogs. I only hope she doesn't go near that nice Mr Cook – he's only recently returned to work after his troubles. They say he never quite got used to all the female attention he received from his time presenting the Big British Cook-Up. Wherever he went, middle-aged women would throw themselves at him, demanding he poke their soggy bottoms. Eventually, he sought solace in illegal substances and hasn't been on national television since. Only just managed to kick the habit, poor chap.

Three o'clock. I don't know what all the fuss is about real ale. I can drink it like tea – I'm sober as a hedge... fudge... judge! Which reminds me, time to pop over to the WI tent to see that dishy Barry Cook judge the baking competition before the fire display and the dog brigade. Can't miss Joan's giant face when I thrash her with my scones!

4.00 p.m. I won't pretend it wasn't a bit of a shock when I heard about the surprise entry in the Women's Institute Baked Teatime Goods category. I've no objection to healthy competition but it all smelt a bit fishy to me. Well, it smelt of something, though I couldn't quite put my finger on what. Naturally, Mr Cook loved my sultana-and-cinnamon buns. But then it was the turn of the so-called reggae reggae scones. Made by some mystery entrant, apparently. He prodded and sniffed them, then he tasted them and started nodding. And nodding. And nodding. Then suddenly he couldn't get enough of them, shovelling them into his silly grinning face like there was no tomorrow. I've never seen anything like it in thirty years.

Four o'clock. Yes!!! You should have seen Joan scowling when I seized victory from out of her big jaws! Barry loved my special scones – giggling like a schoolgirl, he was! No doubt Joan will be asking for another drugs test. Well, it won't change the fact that I beat her, and it won't do Joan any harm to put up with Silver for one year. That's another thing crossed off my bucket list, and it wasn't even on it! Is there no end to my talents? It really is going to be my year after all!

## Sunday 22nd

I've never been more humiliated in my life. Beaten into second place by that 'mystery entrant'. Who turned out to be Bridget, of course! No sooner had Mr Cook announced his decision than she leapt onto the stage to give him a big kiss, sending the poor man fleeing in fear, arms filled with scones. Last anyone saw of him, he'd passed out in a Portaloo.

Then, as my mother always said, 'Just when you think things can't get any worse, you can be sure that things will suddenly get a great deal worse.' It's not a great saying, but it was certainly appropriate in this instance. I was just about to lodge an official objection – most unlike me – when suddenly the tent was filled with a dozen police dogs, followed by their handlers, leaping over demijohns of rhubarb wine and jars of parsnip marmalade, scything down silver-haired amateur chefs and making straight for the few remaining scones. I've no idea what happened next, it was all so fast. Apparently, Bridget shot out of the tent, dogs in hot pursuit, and jumped on her mobility scooter. According to local radio, she somehow managed to steer her way round the hog trials. And the traction engines. And the walking-stick demonstration. She even managed to successfully negotiate the fire brigade's forty-five-degree ramp and Flaming Ring of Death. But her luck finally ran out when the dogs cornered her by the perimeter fence and she attempted to clear it. She may think she's a movie star, but that movie star is definitely not Steve McQueen.

## Monday 23rd

It's so hard to see Bridget lying helpless in a hospital bed, comatose, attached to a drip. I've tried, but visiting hours coincide with *Columbo*.

## Wednesday 25th

Poor Bridget. Just been reading her diary and I'm actually starting to feel sorry for the daft, deluded dumpling. Whichever way she paints it, not much has gone right for her this year. So I've decided to arrange a little surprise for her. I thought she should at least tick one more item off her list so I've booked a short holiday for us next month. I'm sure she'll be out of hospital by then.

## Thursday 26th

Bridget's regained consciousness at last. I think she was happy to see me, although she seemed more concerned with the whereabouts of her mobile phone. I said I imagined it probably ended up inside one of that mystery entrant's special scones. When she finally deigned to speak to me she was quite sombre. She's never been very good with illness and injury and told me she's got a terrible fear of being buried alive. But I think I managed to put her mind at rest. I promised that if she deteriorated I'd turn off her life-support machine as soon as possible, just in case. She only perked up when the doctor informed her she had a case for compensation due to health-and-safety deficiencies at the fete.

## Monday 30th

Bridget's finally been discharged from hospital. Oh well, at least I've finished half of my serial-killers jigsaw – who knew there were so many? It makes you wonder what pushed them over the edge. There can't be that many Bridgets in the world, surely?

# OCTOBER

## Tuesday 1st

So nice to be back where I belong at Joan's side. And she says she's taking me on a little mystery tour this weekend. She told me to pack for three days, so if I start now I should be done by the weekend. Can't say I'm really in the mood for museums and military what-nots but I suppose I should show willing.

## Friday 4th

Five o'clock. Big mystery! Blackpool. I must have been here a hundred times. Can't imagine why Joan would think I'd want to come again, especially at this time of year. She's booked us into some pokey little bed and breakfast on the seafront. No stars, obviously. At least what it lacks in grandeur, it makes up in location. It's less than a hundred yards from the sea. Considerably less when the tide's in. Still, I suppose it saves on having a swimming pool in the front garden.

5.12 p.m. I don't know why Bridget's moaning. My parents always used to bring me here when I was a child and nothing's changed since then. Except possibly a touch of coastal erosion. I hope she perks up soon. Ever since she lost that phone she's been as miserable as sin – I don't think I can cope with being the cheerful one for much longer.

## Saturday 5th

Noon. What a morning! Joan took me for a walk along the front. The sea was awfully choppy and I very nearly got dragged in a few times by rogue waves. I had to hold on to Joan until the danger passed. Luckily she's more sturdy than me even though she's suffered more than her share of erosion herself. Then we went onto the pier. I came over all funny looking down between the planks and had to go for a sit down in the penny arcade.

12.04 p.m. What a morning! Groped by Bridget on the seafront every time she felt the slightest splash of spray. At least the wind took her 'Kiss Me Quick, I Haven't Got Much Time Left' hat. Then she dragged me into the amusement arcade on the pier under the pretext of having one of her funny turns. And then I had to pay for her to go on every blooming machine in the place because she didn't have 'the right change'. The woman takes half the GNP of Switzerland in coppers with her every time she goes to the supermarket but turns up in a penny arcade with a fifty-pound note! If it wasn't for her second funny turn, it would have cost me a small fortune. Not exactly sure what happened but all the colour drained from her face when she was looking into the What the Butler Saw machine. I wonder what came over her? And just when I thought I'd finally managed to cheer her up too.

3.36 p.m. Popped back to the pier while Bridget had a little lie down. Found out exactly what came over her. And what the butler saw! So Bridget did have a career in the movies after all. Well one, at least. She was certainly careering around, anyway. From the dining room to the butler's pantry to the bedchamber to the stables. I've never seen a parlourmaid move so quickly. I hope she got a Christmas bonus. Must remember to check Amazon when we get home to see if it's on DVD. Not that I'd buy a copy, of course. Or show it on residents' film night.

Eight o'clock. Felt a bit better after resting my eyes for a little while. Can't remember what happened. I asked Joan but she was very cagey. I must have a touch of something. I knew I shouldn't have left home. Anyway, Joan's knocking now to drag me off to spend a chilly afternoon on the beach. I don't know how much more of this I can take. I know she means well, but I wish she'd just leave me alone to stare sadly out of the window thinking about my Chuck. Oh well, not too much longer to go, at least.

## Sunday 6th

4.41 p.m. Bridget was terribly subdued on the beach this afternoon. Normally she's prancing about in the surf in her dayglo-pink swimsuit like an epileptic prawn, trying to catch the eye of the lifeguard. This cheering-up business is proving harder work than I anticipated. Although I have to say it was quite amusing when that seagull snatched her 'Kiss Me Quick, Squeeze Me Carefully, I've Got Brittle Bones' hat. And then when that other one flew away with her wig. Actually, the poor woman was quite distressed so I thought I'd better do something to cheer her up. Luckily I'd spotted a candy-floss stall not twenty yards away and in a few minutes she was as right as rain. Until it rained. And her new pink wig melted all down her face.

Quarter to five. I want to go home. Cold, wet and now humiliated. Why is Joan torturing me like this? I thought she was supposed to be my friend. I still don't get why she brought me here in the first place. She said it was something to do with my list but I don't know what she's talking about. That's it. I'm going to bed until it's time to go home tomorrow. Then at least she can't do anything more to make my life a misery.

Half past nine. Joan came knocking on my door again this evening. I told her to leave me alone but she insisted she had something very important she had to show me. Reluctantly, I followed her out of the B&B into the dark and down the road. After a little way, she stopped and looked at her watch. I looked around.

'What's going on?' I asked, a little grumpily. 'Why have you brought me here? Isn't it enough you've hidden my phone, now you're trying to finish me off? Are you planning on pushing me under the next tram?'

'Shush,' she answered. 'We just need to wait a minute.'

'Wait for what?' I said. 'I don't get it. Why are we here?'

'I told you. Just wait,' she answered, curtly.

'No,' I said. 'I mean, why are we *here*? In Blackpool? I've been here hundreds of times. Why did you think this would make me feel better?'

'Ah, but have you ever been at this time of year?' Joan asked.

'Well, no. Of course not. Why would I? It's freezing! I don't get it.'

'I'm afraid my savings didn't quite run to the Arctic Circle,' she said, looking up from her watch, 'so I thought this might do instead.' I followed her gaze. Suddenly the black night was filled with sparkling rocket ships, laughing sailors, the gleaming tower – all aglow with a billion watts of good old-fashioned northern electricity. 'Blackpool Illuminations,' she announced, proudly, 'the real Northern Lights.'

I stared at her, then back at the lights.

'Why Joan…' I said, beaming, 'they're wonderful.'

## Monday 7th

Fingers crossed, I think that little weekend away did the trick. Bridget's back to her irritating old self again. And it did me the power of good too. Went on Amazon and found a DVD entitled *What the Butler Saw*, starring a certain Bridget LaFontaine. It suggested that customers who liked it might also like another DVD, *The Christmas Bonus*. And *Bridget Does Bridlington*.

## Tuesday 8th

Don't know why I bothered taking Bridget all the way to Blackpool. All it took to cheer her up was a nice young policeman with her mobile phone in a plastic bag. Apparently they'd been checking it for calls to Colombia for some reason. He apologised for taking so long to return it as it had only taken a few minutes to confirm that there were no such calls. But a further two weeks for all the boys at the station to finish reading all her highly entertaining and borderline obscene texts. Honestly, a few little messages from that toy boy of hers, and she's out doing pirouettes in the garden. I fear for my prize geraniums.

I'm so excited. I'm so excited. I'm about to lose control – and I think I like it. Chuck has just texted to say he's coming over from America and he can't wait to meet me!

## Wednesday 9th

The only problem is, he wants to meet me at Magnolia Hall. Says he can't wait to see me in my aristocratic surroundings.

Now that I think about it, perhaps I may have been a little bit creative with my username on that website. Well, I suppose I could entertain him here. Mrs Sharples is taking the residents off for a weekend in Milton Keynes. I'll just have to have one of my funny turns and miss the trip. He'll be none the wiser – I'm sure this old place could pass for a stately home with a bit of hard work. Hmmm… I think Joan had better have one of my funny turns too.

## Saturday 12th

Two women have just been carried out of the church hall on stretchers. Bridget must have gone to Zumba without her sports bra again.

## Wednesday 16th

Went to the beauty parlour to prepare for my date with destiny. The beautician suggested I have a vajazzle. I didn't have a clue what she was talking about so I had to ask Joan.

Bridget just asked me what a vajazzle is. I said that on her it would be like putting fairy lights round the Arc de Triomphe.

## Friday 18th

Haven't got time to go to the supermarket this morning – too busy making myself look fabulous for Chuck. I've given Joan a list of all the ingredients for tomorrow night's little dinner. Taken her advice into account and so sticking to a very tight budget.

Shopping List:

Oysters – 2 dozen

Pâté de foie gras – 8 ounces

Steak fillets – 3 (one rare, one medium, one well done, in case)

Oven chips – 1 bag

Saffron – 1 jar (for the gravy)

Napoleon Cognac – 1 bottle (for the trifle)

Champagne – 1 magnum

Powdered rhino horn – 100 grams (for the coffee)

Bad enough having to put up with Bridget being all hoity-toity, now I'm supposed to do all the shopping for her ladyship's so-called romantic soirée. At least it gives me the opportunity to rein her spending in a little. Not that it actually matters what ingredients I buy, they'll all end up burnt, battered or an interesting shade of blue.

## Saturday 19th

Six o'clock. I'm all of a fluster, getting myself ready for tonight. I'm quite certain Chuck will recognise my aristocratic breeding but I don't want to smear Moonlight Serenade mascara all over my designer Holly Willoughby evening gown. Oh, and I must remember to brief Joan fully as to her duties this evening. I don't want my chances ruined by any little slip-ups.

6.08 p.m. I can't believe the things I'll do just to get a little more jigsaw time. Now Her Majesty's got me dressed up in a demeaning uniform to serve dinner for her and her incoming Texan. Not even a proper uniform either, it's a 'Frisky Fifi' French maid's outfit. Oh well, *c'est la vie*.

Half past ten. Such an enjoyable evening. I have to admit I was a little nervous but I needn't have been concerned. Chuck was completely enamoured of me, so much so in fact, he barely touched his food. He was too busy complimenting me on my beautiful eyes and my beautiful home. Even Joan managed to be less surly than usual, playing her part with a grace and coordination I haven't seen since the time she managed to do the hokey-cokey without breaking the sideboard. When the evening finally came to a close, he simply bid me goodbye with a tip of his Stetson and a peck on the cheek, and moseyed off into the sunset. Fingers crossed, it looks like I could have found the love of my life at last! All right, maybe he's not quite as young as he claimed he was, but he's still technically a toy boy.

10.37 p.m. Such an enjoyable evening. Bridget barely had time to put on her tiara when the doorbell rang and I was sent to greet her toy boy. I say toy boy, he must have been nearly as old as her – overpaid, oversexed and over eighty. All that Botox wasn't fooling anyone. Apart from Bridget, it seems, who, once again, flatly refused to wear her spectacles because she says they make her look older. Amazingly, it seemed to work. He fawned all over her all evening, in spite of being unable to swallow a single mouthful of her culinary 'feast'. They got on like a care home on fire. When the evening came to a close – finally – he plonked his ridiculous cowboy hat on his balding head, somehow managed to evade Bridget's slobbering lips and shuffled off into the shrubbery.

## Sunday 20th

What a magical day! Since last night's romantic rendez-vous, I've felt like there's music everywhere I've been. I've completely forgotten to talk to Joan.

What a magical day. I must swap Bridget's hearing aid for an iPod more often.

## Tuesday 22nd

My serial-killers jigsaw is moving on apace since Bridget's beau arrived on the scene. I've done all the edges and most of the sky. Time at last to fill in the rogues' gallery. At this rate, with any luck, I'll be done by Christmas.

## Wednesday 23rd

Lovely, relaxing day with Chuck. Went to the Pencil Case Museum in the morning and Teapotland in the afternoon.

Lovely, relaxing day without Bridget. Finished off Dr Crippen in the morning and the Boston Strangler in the afternoon.

## Friday 25th

Joan's getting very excited about Hallowe'en. It's the only public holiday she does get excited about. She's not much of a one for Christmas – she reckons it's got too religious these days. She's organising a party in the home. We're decorating it to look like a haunted house. So that shouldn't take long. She's even organising some special games, which isn't like her at all, although she insists they'll be fun. I'm not sure about the bobbing for apples – it looks awfully difficult. Joan reckons you have to push your face right down into the water to do it properly. She says that if I have any problems she'll be happy to help. I'm going to the shops tomorrow to get my costume. I've promised to take Joan along to get one too – she's not really one for a needle and thread. Such a shame my Chuck had to fly away suddenly on a business trip. I suppose I'll have to get used to being the trophy girlfriend of a busy executive.

## Monday 28th

Bridget's parading around the living room in her new onesie. I only hope she can get it off quick enough when she needs a twosie.

## Tuesday 29th

Popped into town to get our Hallowe'en costumes this afternoon. Not only did the compensation I received for that accident clear all my debts, but it left me with a tidy sum too – it's amazing how quickly they settled once Joan threatened to sell my story to *Horse & Hound*. Time to spend some of it now. I must say I was very impressed with the range in that new fancy-dress shop – they had all kinds of outfits. Scary but glamorous, like Joan and me. In that order. In the end I managed to find one that should win me the fancy-dress competition, no problem.

That's the last time I let Bridget take me shopping. We ended up in some new shop in the high street called Gran Summers. I've never seen anything like it. I don't know what was worse, the Dormant Rabbit or the Kinky Lollipop Lady outfit. The place was full of all kinds of odd-smelling multicoloured liquids and gels. It was like Bridget's dressing table. It wasn't like any fancy-dress shop I've ever seen before, that's for sure! In the end I had to order my costume online – a good old-fashioned flesh-eating zombie. I only hope it gets here on time.

## Wednesday 30th

All these TV news reports about pensioner-related mug-
gings is making Joan too nervous to go out. She's worried
the police will finally catch her.

## Thursday 31st

Well, that was quite a night! I can't say that Hallowe'en
parties are really my thing – it's difficult to look glamorous
at such a ghoulish event but I think I pulled it off, thanks
to my Sexy Charity Shop Worker costume! I'm not sure
what Joan was in the end. Some kind of zombie, I think.
Sadly, I didn't win the fancy-dress competition but I was
very gracious in defeat, as ever. And in the end, I was still
the winner. In fact, I had a much better prize altogether!

Well, that was quite a night! First, my costume didn't
arrive so I had to host the party in my normal clothes. Then
Bridget tipped the apple-bobbing bowl over the cat because
she didn't win the fancy-dress competition. It was a close
run thing, by all accounts, but in the end it was Enid who
took first prize with her excellent Texas Chainsaw Massacre
Victim costume. Although she was later disqualified when
the judges realised it wasn't a costume.

Things took an unexpected turn later in the evening when the werewolf who had been mauling Bridget all night took off his mask and turned out not to be Mr Gooch, as we'd all assumed, but her 'toy boy'. And, as if that wasn't enough, the next thing we knew he was down on one hairy knee asking her to marry him! Extraordinary. Bridget fainted clean away. It took several minutes and a large sherry to revive her. She finally came to, clutching the diamond ring she'd somehow managed to grab on the way down. Then she grinned a big soppy grin and closed her eyes. I had to slap her several times. She hadn't fainted again, I just had to slap her.

# NOVEMBER

### Friday 1st

I just can't sleep! Last night keeps replaying over and over
again in my mind. All I can see is me and Chuck in the
middle of the dance floor, like Grace Kelly and Prince
Rainier of Monaco.

I just can't sleep! Bridget keeps replaying the night over and
over in my earhole. All I can see is her and that American
in the middle of the dance floor, like the Queen and one
of her corgis.

### Saturday 2nd

Let joy be unconfined! I'm no longer a 'sad, lonely wrin-
kleton with nothing to look forward to but dying alone'.
I am loved, I'm adored by the most wonderful man in the
world, with his own company, his own ranch and his own
teeth! My pacemaker's all a-flutter. I've got love in my eyes,
although that could be glaucoma.

## Monday 4th

Another lovely day with Chuck. After a nice cup of tea, we found a Labrador sanctuary and the American World of Dentures.

Another lovely day without Bridget. After a nice cup of tea, I found Jack the Ripper's pocket watch and Charles Manson's beard.

## Tuesday 5th

Fireworks Night tonight! My favourite night of the year – all those flashes and all that banging. Of course, Joan isn't keen. She gets easily upset at loud noises and people enjoying themselves.

Guy Fawkes Night tonight. Don't know how Bridget can say it's her favourite night of the year – with all those flashes and all that banging, I'm surprised she can distinguish it from any other night.

## Wednesday 6th

Had a very successful day with our Penny for the Guy outside the post office. Probably because it was so realistic. We made twenty-five pounds to put towards Mrs Wilson's funeral.

What a relief Bridget made so much money with her Penny for the Guy. Maybe now she'll let the funeral director have Mrs Wilson's body back.

## Thursday 7th

I thought that Bridget getting together with that cowboy might have calmed her down a bit but she's worse than ever – constantly riffling through the pages of *Blushing Bride* magazine and practising her new signature over and over again. Bridget Dubois – how ridiculous! At least I'm getting even more time alone with my serial killers. Now, what did I do with John Wayne Gacy's moustache…?

## Saturday 9th

Mrs Sharples has just got us one of those new walk-in baths. Can't say that I'm impressed – when I'd done, there was water all over the bathroom floor!

Just explained to Bridget how walk-in baths work. The most important bit being don't walk into one when I'm already in it!

## Wednesday 13th

Yet another wonderful day with Chuck. Got lots done – visited Biscuit World and Dinnington Wiggery, and it was a lovely surprise to come across the Dame Judi Dench Experience in Upper Prestwick.

Yet another wonderful day without Bridget. Got lots done – completed Ted Bundy and the Acid Bath Murderer, and it was a lovely surprise to come across Jeffrey Dahmer hiding under the sideboard.

## Saturday 16th

Dear diary, so sorry I've been neglecting you. I'm afraid another has come between us and completely swept me off my feet. I don't know what I was doing, wasting my time playing bingo, sitting in the television room and going to that silly little park with Joan. And to think of all those custard creams we used to get through together – as Chuck says, a beautiful young woman like me must be careful not to let herself go, especially when her wedding day is on Christmas Eve!

## Monday 18th

The most thrilling part of a girl's wedding is picking the dress. Of course, I couldn't possibly do it without Joan. She'd be devastated to miss out on all that excitement, so I've booked a special appointment for us both at House of Brides with prosecco and peanuts and their head wedding stylist, Bruno. I can only imagine Joan's face when she sees me twirling around the fitting room like the fairy-tale princess she's always imagined me to be!

If Bridget expected me to sit for eight hours while she flounced around in every wedding dress in the shop, she should have given me a bottle of whisky, not a glass of sparkling wine. If it wasn't for the peanuts it would have been a dead loss. And to make matters worse, she insisted on choosing my Matron of Honour dress too: a disturbing mock-Tudor lilac creation complete with silver cape and wimple. Much to Bruno's dismay, she finally settled on a bespoke royal combination for herself: the upper half of Princess Kate's dress and the lower half of Pippa Middleton's.

## Tuesday 19th

Bridget's fiancé keeps giving her late-night booty calls. Although he has to ring at midday so she can get there in time.

Joan's getting terribly agitated about my love life lately. Although to be fair, she gets equally angry about sex, whether it's straight or gay – she's bi-furious.

## Friday 22nd

Just been watching a documentary with Joan about President Kennedy. She says you never forget where you were on the day he was shot. I told her I was busy partying with the Beatles. John Lennon always had the hots for me. He even wrote a song about me!

Bridget reckons John Lennon wrote a song about her. I'm guessing it was 'Give Peace a Chance'.

## Saturday 23rd

Latest wedding update: Bridget wants Westminster Abbey for the service, Paul McCartney and Dame Kiri Te Kanawa to sing 'Bright Eyes' as she walks down the aisle and Bishop Desmond Tutu to officiate. I suspect this is all starting to get a little out of hand.

## Sunday 24th

Chuck's been very helpful with wedding preparations. He's even written a special gift list which he says is befitting of a lady with my aristocratic breeding:

Black satin bedsheets and kimonos

Prada ski jackets

Fabergé egg

Gold-plated teapot

Gucci handbag

Case of champagne

His and hers cashmere bathrobes

Yacht

## Monday 25th

I feel terribly selfish. Poor Joan must have been feeling quite left out of our forthcoming nuptials – she's just offered to be my official wedding planner. But then, I suppose it's the nearest she's going to get to being me. I told her not to scrimp on anything; after all, a girl only gets married six times – and I want this one to last!

Couldn't stand any more of Bridget's wedding talk about jewel-encrusted thrones and purple unicorns – at this rate she'll be bankrupt all over again. So, against my better judgement, I've stepped in to take control.

Revised wedding list:

Rubber bedsheet and commode

Primark anoraks

Kinder egg

Microwave

Bag for life

Crate of brown ale

His and hers polyurethane bath mats

Yoghurt

## Thursday 28th

Went to the doctor's for a medical this morning. Chuck reckons it's compulsory before getting married at our age. He's even got some special forms for me to sign when I get back.

Bridget just asked me to help her read through some life-insurance forms Chuck has given to her to sign. You'd have thought he'd be too busy thinking about the wedding – seems a bit odd to me. I even had to take Bridget to have a medical although it doesn't take long at her age. These days the doctor just holds a mirror under her nose.

# DECEMBER

## Sunday 1st

December! Not long until Christmas Eve! To think that this time next year I'll be looking forward to a Texan Christmas, whatever that entails. Barbecued turkey, no doubt. Just been watching *It's a Wonderful Life*. Such a heart-warming story – a man being shown by an angel what the world would have been like if he'd never been born. Joan refuses to watch it. She says there's no point in wasting time on silly romantic fantasies. I wonder what life would have been like for Joan if I hadn't been born? It doesn't bear thinking about.

I can't stand watching *It's a Wonderful Life*. And I can't bear to think about what my life would have been like if Bridget had never been born. No point in wasting time on silly romantic fantasies.

## Monday 2nd

I must say, my wedding-dress diet is going very well indeed!

Food consumed today:

Ryvitas (4) – 76 calories

Tea with lemon (2 cups) – zero calories

Pilchards in tomato sauce (1 tin) – 125 calories

Salad (as much as I like) – zero calories

Small low-fat yoghurt (1) – 150 calories

Total calories – 351.

Jumping for joy!

If Bridget's hoping to fit into that tiny wedding dress, she'll have to do better on her diet than she has so far!

Food Bridget consumed today:

Custard creams (1 packet) – 1,300 calories

Cups of tea with full cream milk (12) – 252 calories

Large fish, chips and mushy peas with a battered sausage and bread and butter – 2,352 calories

Chocolate eclairs (3) – 780 calories

Total calories – 4,684

She won't be jumping for anything after that lot.

## Wednesday 4th

A terrible to-do today. The television reception was awful all day. I missed *The Wizard of Oz* and *A Perry Como Christmas Turkey*! Turned out it was just Enid on the roof threatening to throw herself off. She must have knocked the aerial while she was up there – terribly thoughtless. Mrs Sharples asked Joan to try and get her down because she's so calm and level-headed. And has an air rifle.

## Monday 9th

Two weeks to go until Bridget Golightly becomes Mrs Bridget Golightly-Dubois the Third! I wonder how Joan is getting on with all the preparations. Haven't heard much from her lately. I hope she's remembered to order enough flowers to fill Westminster Abbey.

## Tuesday 10th

Funny, I've been so preoccupied with my impending nuptials, I've barely thought about Christmas. Normally as soon as summer's gone, it's all I can think about. The only sad thing about Christmas as you get older is that you receive fewer and fewer Christmas cards each year.

The only good thing about Christmas when you get older, is that you have fewer and fewer Christmas cards to write.

## Friday 13th

I've never been much of a one for superstitions, but I knew I shouldn't have talked to Joan about her plans for my wedding on Friday the thirteenth. Never mind Westminster Abbey, she hasn't even booked Desmond Tutu! I should never have left the most important day of my life in her big clumsy hands. How can she expect Chuck and me to get married in that awful register office on the other side of town? How humiliating! I don't know how I'm going to look Paul McCartney in the face.

## Monday 16th

Chuck's terribly thoughtful. He's always asking if I feel all right and joking about me lasting through the honeymoon. I told him he's got no worries on that score – I only hope that he can keep up with me!

Just walked in on Bridget and Chuck. He was testing her blood pressure and asking if there was any history of heart disease in her family. She reckons he's terribly thoughtful, although I'm beginning to wonder exactly what it is he's thinking about.

## Wednesday 18th

At this time of year, Mrs Pettit always seems to get obsessed with poverty, illness and death. So we've put on a heart-warming made-for-TV Christmas film so she can get all three at once.

## Friday 20th

Bridget just asked me if I minded her not leaving me anything in her will. Normally I would have been delighted, considering most of her possessions look like they've been foraged from a Lidl skip. Don't know why but I can't help feeling that Texan is behind this. Perhaps I'd better have a little word while Bridget's having her toenails customised tomorrow, just to ease my concerns.

## Saturday 21st

I'm dumbfounded! Chuck's just told me he was confronted by Joan in the vestibule. Apparently she has some kind of problem with him, although he's no idea what. Well, if she's got a problem with him, she's got a problem with me! What with this and her so-called 'arrangements', it's clear she's trying to sabotage our wedding. And I told her so in no uncertain terms. I said if Chuck isn't welcome in this home, then she isn't welcome at our wedding!

## Tuesday 24th

Ten o'clock. The big day has arrived. Not as big as I'd hoped, thanks to Joan, but at least whatever happens, by the end of the day I'll be a married woman. And it's just started to snow so hopefully the register office won't look too horrendous in the photographs.

10.04 a.m. The big day has arrived! The day I finally finish my jigsaw, now I don't have to go to this ridiculous charade of Bridget's. Just a few pieces to go now. There's the Preston Poisoner's foot… and there's Stan the Slasher's bloody cleaver. Just one serial killer left, now where's he gone? Oh well, I'll look for it after I've made a quick cup of tea for me and… oh, just me. Well, that should be even quicker then.

1.15 p.m. Finally found the missing piece of the jigsaw! It was down the back of the sofa all the time with Bridget's spare dentures and the cat. And so the jigsaw is, at last, complete! Funny, that Stetson looks awfully familiar. I'll check the box…

'The Texas Toy Boy, 1930–present. Notorious fraudster, philanderer and murderer of wealthy, aristocratic elderly women. STILL AT LARGE.'

Not if I've got anything to do with it, he won't be! I knew I recognised him from somewhere – must have been *America's Most Wanted*. I'd better ring the police. I only hope they can make it in time!

1.53 p.m. What a ride! Racing across town through the driving snow, charging through red lights, swerving at the last minute to avoid present-laden shoppers and drunken revellers, barely missing garland-strewn lamp posts and fairy-lit Christmas trees, weaving between vehicles, onward, ever onward, through howling gales and blinding blizzards until finally I parked my mobility scooter and burst through the register-office doors. But I was too late.

## Wednesday 25th

Quietest Christmas Day I can remember. No charades, no enforced carolling, but at least pulling my own cracker meant not having to rummage round on all fours to find the plastic frog. I even got to watch the whole of *The Great Escape* in peace. No doubt about it, Christmas Day without the sound of Bridget is a very different experience.

## Thursday 26th

Quiet Boxing Day too. In spite of myself, I'm starting to miss Bridget's inane chatter filling up the day. But if she doesn't want to talk to me, that's her lookout. And it does give me time to catch up on my box-sets.

## Friday 27th

Still quiet. That's four days now. I can't help wondering what's going on in that little mind of hers. Mainly because I've run out of jigsaws. She hasn't said a word since I picked her up from the police station, mascara running down her face, over her wedding dress and onto the taxi floor. She's always worn a lot of mascara. There was no sign of Mr Dubois the Third. The desk sergeant reckoned he'd get life, which by my reckoning, for him, is around two to three years.

## Monday 30th

6.12 p.m. That's it, I've had enough. Straight after dinner, I'm going up to her room to have it out with her once and for all. She's not giving ME the silent treatment, whether I want it or not!

7.20 p.m. Went up to Bridget's room to find it empty. She'd gone to the lavatory. As usual. As I sat there waiting for her to return, my eyes were irresistibly drawn to the bedside table, on which lay her diary, for all the world to see. Well, it would have been rude not to have a look…

'Betrayed! How could Joan do this to me? Couldn't she let me have my moment of happiness, after all the years of selfless support and friendship I've given her? To ruin my wedding day like that with her petty suspicions. Poor Chuck, he'd barely pulled his mother's ring from his pocket before the register-office doors flew open and twenty burly policemen raced in and leapt on him. What's going to become of me now? Stuck here in this miserable place for the rest of my life, my heart broken and my dreams shattered.'

## Tuesday 31st

Ten o'clock. Was just going to make myself a cup of tea when my door creaked opened and Joan stepped into the room. She didn't say anything. She just sat heavily on the bed next to me, put her arm around my shoulders and we both gave each other the silent treatment for a little while longer. Then, we were ready to talk.

11.00 a.m. Finally explained everything to Bridget. It wasn't easy, but these things never are – it took me three days to explain to her how the toaster worked. In the end, she seemed to understand what had happened and why I'd felt I had to call the police and eventually, after a few tears, she even managed a little wonky smile. Then suddenly she jumped up with a start and raced downstairs. I followed her, baffled as ever, to the Christmas tree in the hall. After some rummaging, she finally emerged from beneath its needleless branches and handed me a shiny red package tied up with a big gold bow. She rocked impatiently from foot to foot as, with a sense of trepidation, I slowly unwrapped it. To my great surprise, it wasn't a limited edition Dolly Parton collectors' plate or an emerald-encrusted toilet brush.

'Do you like it, Joan?' she said, her little eyes twinkling with childish glee. 'I know that sometimes you haven't always been that keen on my gifts but this time I wanted to give you something you'd really love.'

I have to say, words failed me. Amazingly, there it

was: a hand-crafted two-thousand-piece wooden jigsaw. Of Bridget.

Quarter past nine. I'm so pleased. Joan was so overwhelmed with my Christmas present that she had to have a little sit down to compose herself. I gave her a few minutes before I asked her where mine was. She blinked back another tear before disappearing to her room and returning to hand me a small book-shaped gift. I'm so glad that we're friends again. I eagerly ripped off the paper to find...

'Oh Joan, it's lovely, but I don't really think diary writing's for me, after all. It just seems to get me into trouble.'

'Don't worry, Bridget,' she said. 'It's not a diary.'

'But then, what is it?' I asked, confused.

'Take a closer look,' she said, so I did.

'A travel journal?' I said, even more confused.

'Yes,' said Joan. 'To get you into even more trouble.'

'But I don't understand,' I said.

'You will,' she answered, a smug grin forming on her big face. She took my little hand in hers and led me out of the door and down the gravel path to the bottom of the garden. 'Happy Christmas,' she said, pulling back the shed door to reveal a most unusual contraption. I stared at it for some time and then back up at Joan.

'It's lovely,' I said. 'But whatever is it?'

'I've been working on it for a while,' she replied. 'It's a mobility scooter... made for two.'

I looked at it again. It was the most beautiful thing I'd ever seen.

'Well, don't just stand there,' she said, handing me a glistening helmet with a big letter B on it. 'Hop on.'

I climbed aboard and she turned the key.

'But where are we going, Joan?' I asked.

'Wherever the road takes us,' she said. 'Just sit back and enjoy the ride.' She smiled down at me and I smiled back.

So, at last, this is it. No turning back. No more Mrs Sharples. No more bland, liquidised dinners. No more sitting in a dusty room full of high-backed chairs, listening to the sound of snoring and the clock ticking. No more having to watch Mr Gooch readjust himself during *Countdown*. No more grey days in grey rooms with grey people. There's a bright, colourful world out there and it's ours for the taking! At least, until the battery needs recharging...

# THE END?